soulmates
and other stories

169 there to this
168 change Move to moved

AN ANTHOLOGY OF SHORT STORIES

soulmates

and other stories

R.K. Simpson

**The New
Atlantian Library**

THE NEW ATLANTIAN LIBRARY
is an imprint of
ABSOLUTELY AMAZING eBOOKS

Published by Whiz Bang LLC, 926 Truman Avenue, Key West, Florida 33040, USA.

ISBN 978-1-951150-05-1

For information contact:
Publisher@AbsolutelyAmazingEbooks.com

This book is dedicated to the memory of Master Sergeant Tom Saunders, United States Marine Corps.

soulmates

and other stories

Table of Contents

SOULMATES

I was sipping a Coke at the Orlando Airport, waiting to board my flight back to Boston, when I glanced at the television and saw her face for the first time in more than twenty years. The mug shot made her look considerably older than I, but it was my high school girlfriend, I was quite sure. Then, over the din in the bar, I heard the newscaster say, "Ms. Chloe MacLaren, the dead man's daughter, is a person of interest in the case." Hearing that news was shocking, but deep down I was not entirely surprised.

When I knew Chloe, two internal forces seemed to be battling to control her. The dominant Chloe was difficult to know and impossible to understand. She operated on impulse much of the time, which made her unpredictable. She disliked schedules, did not make lists, and never wore a watch. This Chloe was an introvert who disliked people but had developed an extraordinary ability to manipulate them. She could make a positive impression on the most skeptical and discerning, and always got what she wanted, one way or the other.

The subordinate Chloe fought constantly to keep her humanity from being trampled. Because she loved animals, especially horses, she had volunteered at a large-animal clinic since she was fourteen. The same protective instinct drove her to look after her friends. In my case, throughout our senior year she never missed an opportunity to point out why I needed a college education. She is, no doubt, the primary reason I now have a Master's degree in Spanish and have been able to find work easily. She even talked her father into lending me money to pay school bills when funds from my scholarships and work were insufficient.

I liked her father, Jock MacLaren, from the first time I met him. Known to all as Scotty, he was a man of few words and subtle wit. After watching one of Florida's long-winded governors on television, he shook his head, fixed me with those piercing blue eyes, and said, "Remember, you never

1

learn anything when you're talking." At 5' 6", he stood ramrod straight on bowed legs. He had close-cropped red hair, an aquiline nose, and small blue eyes that looked into you, not at you. He was smart and shrewd and if anyone could have figured out his daughter, it was he. But those two strong-willed, stubborn, personalities were a volatile mix. One word could spark an argument between them and sometimes it did. It was a damned shame.

I had never spoken to Chloe until the first day of our senior year when Fate dropped me into a chair right behind hers. She was wearing a yellow sundress that revealed toned and tanned arms and shoulders and enough of the tops of her breasts to make me hope every morning she would wear that dress again. Her reddish-brown hair was cut boyishly short and her nose was too long for her face, but her beautiful eyes drew attention from it. Their delicate color seemed to change from grey to green to grey-blue depending on her surroundings. And like a cat's eyes, they saw everything and revealed nothing.

As soon as I sat down, Chloe turned around in her seat, extended her hand, and said, "You're Sandor Rigor, right? Do you prefer Sandy?"

"Either," I said.

Despite having little in common, I think she selected me to be her senior-year toy that morning. We were so different that some kids referred to us as "the odd couple." Chloe was a member of the in-crowd, while I stayed as far from that group as I could and indiscriminately disliked every kid in it. Chloe's family had money; we had none. Chloe was a diligent student motivated to do her best always. I was a lackadaisical, unmotivated, pain-in-the-ass student. The teachers who knew me considered me an under-achiever because, according to the IQ test we took at the beginning of our sophomore year, mine was an impressive 130.Chloe did not consider me an under-achiever, however, which was more important to me, because from the first time we slept together we were in perfect synch.

We did share one other thing, something that was much less common then than it is now: each of us was an only child being raised by a single parent. We believed we were the only ones in school who understood how difficult the loss of a parent was, how far-reaching and long-lasting the loss was, and how strong the urge was to be just normal kids again. We felt a powerful bond and believed that surviving all we had gone through made us soulmates.

~ ~ ~

Several weeks after seeing Chloe's face on the news, I received a call from a high school classmate. "Sandor, this is a voice from your past. Anthony Gonzalez. Remember me?"

"Yes, of course, Anthony. Que pasa, amigo?"

"Well, you know, it's about Scotty's ... death," he stammered. "My dad used to work for Scotty. He really idolized him. He told great stories about Scotty all the time at home. After high school, when I didn't know what I wanted to do and didn't have a job, Scotty hired me to work in the stables. He talked to me often about life and problem-solving and he helped get me pointed in the right direction. To tell you the truth, his death has really been difficult for me." He paused, took a deep breath and continued. "Then, I remembered that you knew him quite well too, and thought it would be good to talk to you." Anthony's answer left me waiting for more explanation and more candor.

"Yes, I knew him well," I said, without elaborating. "What can you tell me about his death, Anthony?" I asked.

"Well, here's what I know for sure. He died when he was thrown from his horse, Lucky. There were rumors that he had had some heart troubles. Maybe he had a heart attack; maybe he should not have been riding. I'm not sure. I do know that a female friend of Chloe was riding with them that morning. And lastly, I know the press is beginning to publish all kinds of unsubstantiated shit. My father says that's what happens when rich men die."

"How much was he worth? Any idea?"

"That guy just had a knack for making money, Sandor. One article estimated he was worth twenty million.

"Holy shit!" I blurted. "So that's what she inherited?"

"I don't know, but that's generally the way it works. She's an only child. Now she's a rich only child."

"Is there something I can do for you, Anthony?"

"No, not really," he said, unconvincingly. He hesitated and I waited. Finally, he said, "Look, if Scotty was killed, I would hate to see the murder covered up. I know you are smart, and I thought you might feel like I do. That's all. If I can do anything, let me know. I know some people."

"Comprendido," I said. "Don't worry, Anthony, we're on the same wavelength. I can feel it. Would you mind sending me the articles you mentioned that were full of rumors?" I asked.

"Absolutely. I've saved them all and I'll send you new ones as I see them."

"And it might be helpful if you could confirm the heart rumors and find out the name of Chloe's friend who went riding with them that day?"

"I'll try, Sandor."

~ ~ ~

Anthony said two things that piqued my interest. First, he said Scotty had been bucked off his horse. While that was theoretically possible, in reality, it was hard to imagine. Everyone who worked on that ranch had been in awe of his horsemanship. He was strong, agile, and decisive, just what a horse needs to avoid disaster. Plus, Scotty had ridden Lucky for a decade. He knew her every mood and move, and she knew if he had gained a pound or two or was wearing new boots. I knew in my bones that Scotty was not killed by his horse. He was killed by a person.

Second, I could not stop thinking of Chloe's twenty-million-dollar inheritance. I sat there for some time in my one-bedroom rental unit, looking out my dirty front window at the traffic crawling along Route 29 and past a non-descript used car lot. God Almighty! Twenty million dollars!

I mused that if that amount ever fell into my hands, the first thing I would do would be take my mother house shopping. Then I would explain that working in the bar had just become optional. "Do whatever you want Mom," I would say. "You've earned it many times over." What a great feeling that would be!

My mother, Nancy Lancaster, had little education because

around her tenth birthday, she started working in the vegetable and flower farms where her mother worked. She was a wholesome, blond, blue-eyed gal who, by the time she was in her mid-teens, found it easy to get work as a waitress. When she turned eighteen, she graduated to bartender, and that became her life's work. The pay seemed good to her when she started because she learned how to entice big tips and she could work until midnight most nights. But those many years on her feet had contributed to her arthritic knees and back. The longer I thought about it, the more certain I was: it was time for my mother to live in her own place and treat herself to some rest and relaxation.

And so, it was that I began to consider seriously the idea of siphoning off some of Chloe's grotesquely large inheritance for my mother – and me. As I began to weigh the risks involved, I realized my greatest concern – maybe fear – was Chloe. I felt that dread of intimidation return when I recalled her quick temper, her relentlessness, and her cold-hearted determination. If I went after her money, I would have to face those qualities and the fact that, ultimately, it would be me against her, no holds barred winner take all. Could I force her to submit to me? To do my bidding? I had never been able to before, but I was so insecure back then that I had a recurring dream in which Chloe made me do things I knew were wrong or dangerous. We talked about it once and she admitted that she would love to have that kind of power over people because she would enjoy seeing how they reacted, especially to danger. She was frightening sometimes when she spoke her intimate little truths like that, but I was about to learn that her actions could be even more frightening.

The incident began Friday evening. We had gone to a pep rally for the high school football game the next day. I was so nervous I felt sick. I had promised myself I would tell Chloe I was not happy with our relationship. And so I did. Without any preamble, I said, "You're so demanding, Chloe. I try so hard to keep you happy that I'm not happy myself." This announcement caught Chloe absolutely by surprise.

"What the hell are you talking about?" she shot back.

"I was attracted to you, like I was to the pep rally fire

5

tonight," I told her, using a line I had thought up and rehearsed in bed the previous night. "If I saw an orange glow in the night sky, I would alter course and go to it; I couldn't help myself. It was like that when I met you. I was drawn to you. You were like a beautiful fire." Up to that point, she was listening, but then I said, "But now I feel I'm too close to you for my own good, that I have to keep my wits about me or you might draw me in one step too close to the fire and little Sandor would be nothing but ashes in the wind." In reply, she told me what I could do with my ashes, got out of my mother's ancient car, and slammed the door so hard I thought she had broken it.

I anticipated a long silence from Chloe and was surprised when she called on Sunday. She sounded fine and in the most courteous terms invited me to the ranch that afternoon to ride. It was the type of invitation you cannot easily turn down, so I accepted with the hope that we would find some time and privacy to continue our last conversation in a more civilized tone.

During most of the thirty-minute drive to the ranch, I thought about Chloe. Despite the material things her father's financial successes brought her, life had been lonely for her. She had lost her mother, Samantha, when she was fourteen months old to the most brutal killing that ever occurred in Kissimmee. She was raped and murdered while walking home from the movies. Her killer was never found and Scotty – I am sure he would agree – never fully recovered.

For several weeks after Sam died, Scotty stayed in his house, spoke to no one, and contemplated suicide, recording his thoughts on this alternative solution in a small notebook he carried with him at all times. One morning before daybreak, he walked down the hall to his daughter's room, stood by her crib, and was entranced by her quiet, rhythmic breathing. He studied a wisp of blond hair that fluttered each time she exhaled, and he consciously absorbed every aspect of the peaceful expression on her face. He had no idea how long he stood there but at some point, he felt the tension in his neck lessen and the vice that had gripped his chest loosen slightly. Even the anger and sorrow that had caused his worst suffering began to diminish. During that time of solitude and contemplation, Scotty decided not to take his life.

He told me this story one evening driving home from a tennis tournament Chloe played in. These memories affected Scotty so deeply that he had to pull off the road and collect himself. I had to pull off at a gas station myself that morning on my way to the ranch because my mind was on Scotty and Chloe, not the road. I sat in the car with a cup of coffee and wished that all three of us could start again.

Scotty was thirty-five years old when Samantha died. He was already one of the wealthiest and most influential ranchers in central Florida, and he had just been elected President of the Florida Cattlemen's Union. For six months or more after his loss, Scotty struggled with depression. Mornings were the worst time of day. Often his first thought was 'Sam's gone.' This hit him so hard sometimes that he could not get out of bed. Other mornings he was awakened by the shattering thought that her killer was still on the loose and maybe lived around the corner where he was free to enjoy his life.

Of course, time helped them heal. A year or two into her teens, Chloe's highs and lows began to even out, and she took up tennis and riding. Her athletic successes brought her social standing and confidence, but she remained edgy and demanding with Scotty. She just wanted to spend time with him, but it seemed to her that he always chose a meeting with a businessman over an ice cream with her. It made her furious that she could not control him, not even an hour of his day. In turn, her outbursts made him angry and exasperated and their relationship spiraled downward. By the time I arrived in her life, she was seventeen and was essentially estranged from her father. In one of our first serious conversations I remember Chloe saying, "I admire him in some ways, I really do, but I hope to God I don't turn out to be like him. A week later Scotty allowed me my first glance into the state of their relationship when he said, "I am already mourning her loss."

It is impossible to say what kept father and daughter apart. Perhaps it was some genetic disconnect or psychological block Scotty developed as a result of his wife's violent death. I believe Scotty cared for her deeply, although he could not always show it. Chloe, on the other hand, was as cold-blooded as a snake. I never saw Chloe demonstrate a need for human warmth or the ability to generate it.

I arrived at the MacLaren ranch that morning a little late for my riding date. I turned off the main road and onto two sandy grooves in the zoysia grass that ran for about half a mile between two rows of graceful Norfolk Pines. I saw her in the corral, bridle in one hand and blanket in the other, running after a big, black horse. When I pulled to a halt, she dropped the gear, jogged to the car, and said, "I'd like to put Friday behind us as fast as we can."

"Done," I replied, feeling cowardly. She bent down, extended her head and shoulders through the open window and kissed me on the lips. "Take that, cowboy," she grinned.

Shortly thereafter, while walking to the barn, Chloe said, "I think Tetu'll be a good horse for your first ride. He's young and very responsive." I knew next to nothing about horses, but I knew Tetu was a thoroughbred and, therefore, might be high strung, or easily spooked. At first glance he looked enormous. His coat, mane, and tail were jet black, and his opaque black eyes seemed to obscure his attitude and intentions.

Chloe gave me several pointers as she expertly put on his bridle, placed the bit in his mouth, and wrapped the reins around a hitching post. "A horse will move away from pressure," she said, as she threw a blanket over Tetu's back. "So, Rule #1 is: stay relaxed. Hands, arms, ankles, legs – all relaxed. If you're tense, he'll pick up mixed signals which could confuse him." As she spoke, she was trying to tighten the cinch around the horse's girth, but Tetu acted irritable and resisted Chloe's efforts.

"You little devil," she said to Tetu.

"What's the matter?" I asked.

"Well, Mr. Greenhorn, if the cinch isn't tight, the saddle will roll off his back and you'll roll onto on the ground. To make matters worse, Tetu has learned to inhale deeply just before I tighten the cinch. This expands his rib cage. After I have the saddle on him, he expels that air so the cinch won't be so tight. Pretty smart, eh?" But I have a trick of my own," she said. "Let's see if it works." With that she turned toward the horse's flank and drove her knee up into his belly so hard that he expelled a big whoosh of air. Simultaneously, Chloe tightened the cinch and Tetu laid his ears back, switched his tail, and gave Chloe a look that needed no explanation. But the cinch was tight and the saddle secure.

"Sorry," she said to me. "It didn't hurt him – just got his attention."

"You should apologize to him, not me," I suggested.

"You mount up now and let's see what happens," she said, with a touch of impatience in her voice. She handed me the reins.

"Wait a sec," I said, searching for the stirrups with the toes of my sneakers, but Tetu was moving. He walked briskly by the hitching post. Then, without warning, he was in a full gallop, flying around the corner of the barn. He missed driving my knee into it by a fraction of an inch. He banked hard to the left, shot along a fence and began to increase his speed. I have no idea what I did during our speed run, other than maintain my two-handed death grip on Tetu's mane. I do remember my breathing coming in ragged gasps. Suddenly Tetu veered away from the fence and, still at full speed, headed straight for the side of the barn. I was sure that in his crazed state he was going to run right through it. I tried to make myself small and crouch behind his head and neck, but about two feet from impact, he stopped short and I flew over his neck and head like a champagne cork exploding out of the bottle. I hit the barn back first and upside down.

Although I do not remember what happened next, on-lookers said I bounced to my feet instantly and threw a right cross with every ounce of strength available in me while letting out a hair-raising scream. The punch landed flush on the middle of Tetu's upper lip, one of the most sensitive parts of a horse's anatomy, I learned later. Tetu reacted to the pain, noise and surprise of it all by bucking and snorting like a rodeo bronc. Then he took several steps backward, whirled around and charged into the corral. I last saw him galloping away from me and thought, 'He's going in the right direction.'

My mouth was full of corral dirt. I also had a bloody nose

and two sore wrists. Someone handed me a bucket of water and said, "Here,

Sandy, wash your mouth out. You okay?" Then I heard an older hand say, "They shoulda sent that crazy bastard to the glue factory long ago! He's gonna kill someone."

Chloe walked up then and took over. "Okay, thanks folks, break it up – think we've got everything under control."

"Are you okay? Do you need to go to the hospital?"

"I'm okay, I think."

"How'd you like to go for a nice horseback ride?" she asked. I flashed her an unamused smile. "Let's go over to the house."

We sat in the living room, close but not touching, silent much of the time, brooding over what had happened and what might have happened. When I closed my eyes, images from the afternoon slid into and out of focus. The more I saw, the closer I came to relive the entire incident. Chloe, the horse expert, had been dead wrong. Tetu was neither young nor responsive. I missed something she was saying, then tuned in again.

"... and I've cinched him that way for years. Anthony Gonzalez showed me that trick."

I knew Anthony from school. He had worked at the ranch for less than six months. Didn't Chloe know that and why had she insisted that I ride that thoroughbred?

The physical repercussions of the ride were making themselves known. I was nauseous and dizzy and felt like I was coming down with the flu. And I could not shake the image of those menacing empty, black eyes. "I've got to go, Chloe," I said and climbed off the sofa. "I don't feel so great." As I stood, all the fog suddenly blew away. All my questions had answers. "Holy shit!" I stopped and stared at Chloe.

"What?" she asked.

"You arranged that disaster, didn't you? It all makes sense now. You set me up, man! Your invitation. That big kiss. Making me ride that thoroughbred nut case and kicking him in the stomach just before you put me on his back. It was all thought out in advance. You could have killed me!" I grabbed her by the upper arm and jerked her so hard both her feet came off the floor. "I oughta kick your ass," I snarled.

"You don't have the cojones," she said. I watched as big tears ran down both sides of her face, but she made no noise. They were tears of anger not sadness. Then, POOF, the teenager was gone, and an irrational woman was shouting at me. "You're nothing more than a little mama's boy, Sandor. You don't have the backbone to survive in this world. You little piss ant." I listened briefly, hoping she would pause so I could toss in my two cents, but she was gaining momentum and slipping beyond reason. So, I walked out the door and did not see her again until that day in the bar at the Orlando airport.

I never saw Scotty again either, although I did stay in touch with him. For over five years, we called each other regularly and talked about everything under the sun. It was as if he had found a son, and I, a father. The better I knew him, the more I liked him. The only aberration in our relationship was that neither of us ever mentioned Chloe.

~ ~ ~

Three days after our last phone call, an envelope arrived at my post office box full of speculative articles. The reporters must have had fun making up stories about Chloe's many affairs, her lost inheritance, and her role pushing illicit horse drugs. I did glean some useful nuggets from articles in the more reputable papers: Chloe had been a pro tennis player, had acquired three DWI's, and had changed her home address to 555 Padgett Circle in Ocala. As a bonus, Anthony had written "Gladys Montoya, horsewoman," on a piece of paper and put it in the envelope. No mention was made of Scotty's alleged heart condition.

~ ~ ~

The time had come to make a decision about the possibility of relieving Chloe of some of her inheritance. My preliminary thoughts swept away the fantasy that somehow, I could do this without breaking the law. To supplement my income as a Spanish language teacher, I had worked part-time as a bank teller, as an assistant parole officer in a juvenile detention center, and as an Emergency Medical Technician. In those jobs I met folks who were familiar with life on the wrong side of the law. I had never been there myself, but to my surprise, I was not deterred by it. In fact, it seemed to bring clarity to my thinking and resolve not to overlook a single detail. After all, blackmail carried a punishment of 2-15 years in Florida.

I arose early the next morning, made a double-espresso, and went for a long walk with my notebook and pen. When a question or idea occurred to me, good or bad, I wrote it down. When my idea pool dried up, I would run for five minutes then pop a piece of hard candy in my mouth. This seemed to jump-start my creative juices. Afternoon: lunch, nap, shower, and walk. I went to bed early that evening, arose well-rested at six, and started again. By the end of day two, I felt reasonably sure Chloe would be vulnerable to the type of proposal I was considering, especially if she lived alone. Maybe Anthony knew or could find out if she had a husband or partner.

A friend had suggested that I use his summer house for a few days, so I drove to Vermont early the next morning. By ten o'clock I had taken a dip in the cold lake at the foot of his property, eaten a bowl of cereal, and sat myself down on the warm slats at the end of the dock. I was anxious about how I would initially communicate with Chloe, but my subconscious had been at work. It pointed out that I would be harder to find and, God forbid, to convict, if I left behind no sign that I had ever contacted her. If I could watch Chloe's house for signs of life or for Chloe herself, I would not have to contact her beforehand. This revelation was critical to my overall scheme, and when I left the cabin Sunday night, I had the framework of a good plan in mind.

~ ~ ~

The next time I talked to Anthony he sounded genuinely shook up when I told him that Chloe might have killed her father. He also gave me a copy of an assessment he wrote of the new District Attorney. It was an excellent piece of work and I knew it would help me sound knowledgeable and well-connected when I talked to Chloe about her money – and mine. I did not ask Anthony if Chloe lived alone because I did not want him to think I had any interest in rekindling my high school feelings for her. I did ask if Chloe were single or attached. Anthony said he did not know but would try to find out.

~ ~ ~

The next step was to consult my friend Arturo Lena, whose family, according to rumor, was connected to the Mob. I had never asked him about that, of course. A week after returning from Vermont, I went to Art's house ostensibly to watch a Red Sox game, but really to find out how to obtain some fake drivers' licenses. Art handled this request like Johnny Pesky handled a two-bouncer to third. "Here's a number," he said when he realized *I* wanted the driver's licenses. "Call it when you're ready to go there, not before. When they ask who sent you, the answer is Nicky Silverthorne. Be thorough in explaining to them what you want because they can make a driver's license for one hundred bucks that'll withstand no scrutiny or they'll take some dead guy and give you his whole identity, which will withstand a credit check for a mortgage and more. That will run you a lot more, of course. They will call you back with a price and won't start work until you approve. It's cash only, not negotiable, and it won't be cheap."

"One question," I said. "Are these guys dangerous?"

"Just do what you're told. *Capisci?* Don't ask no questions, don't tell no jokes. These people ain't hired for their sense of humor." The next morning, I called the number Art had given me, mentioned his code name, and took my first step in implementing my plan.

The process by which I obtained my documentation took a month and almost emptied my paltry savings account. Getting to their 'studio' involved walks, subway trips, and a fifteen-minute taxi ride while blindfolded. Once there, a nondescript man took my ten grand for the package of documents that, he promised, would withstand scrutiny. They took pictures of me in my three disguises and showed me my new briefcase with three secret compartments for my three identities. Finally, an androgynous little person wearing tinted glasses and a hat spent an hour instructing me how to wear my disguises and use the documentation. "Never wear your disguises close to home. Your neighbors know your gait and your posture, which enables them to see right through your wig, glasses, and clothing. To disguise your walk, wrap an ace bandage tightly around your left knee for one disguise; wrap it around your right foot and ankle for a different disguise. Also, I suggest a lockable toilet stall for changing identities, and you should wear your disguises for several days before using them for real. As you get used to them, you will realize that you do not stand out while wearing this gear and that most people will pay you less attention while you're wearing a disguise. Buy yourself several different styles of hats and jackets. Put them in an easily accessible place. The colors must be muted. Remember, you're trying to blend in, not attract attention to yourself."

The second step in implementing my plan involved acquiring a good lawyer in the Cayman Islands. I did this by contacting the U.S. Interests Section in the British Embassy in Washington. After frustrating delays, I was given telephone numbers for two "esteemed" law offices. I chose one simply because I liked the sound of his name, Jordan Jarett.

Once in phone contact with him, I asked Mr. Jarett about the talk I was hearing that the islands were under increasing pressure to loosen their bank secrecy agreements. Mr. Jarett assured me there would be many more years of talk before that happens. "They have been too good to all of us and to people like you for us to hurriedly dismantle them down," he said in his cultured Caribbean-British accent. Within three weeks I had opened an account in the name of Bert E. Barnett. There was no fee for opening Mr. Barnett's account, but I put five thousand in it, on the theory that the bank should make at least as much as Mr. Jarett had made for mailing Mr. Barnett some forms and then turning them into the office of the Secretary of State of the Cayman Islands.

Having decided that I would not return to my apartment in Boston, I moved my few belongings to a storage locker and dropped off a check for the pro-rated amount of the month's rent under the super's door with an extra hundred dollars for him. There was nothing in the fridge, so I unplugged it, along with all the other appliances, and cancelled my post office box. My final act was to take out the last bag of garbage. With all the loose ends tied off, I set out for Ocala, Florida, over 1200 miles south. It was a long trip, but I vowed to stay under the speed limit all the way. My fake documents were impressive, but I did not want to test them.

~ ~ ~

My first night on the road, I called Anthony from a pay phone in the lobby of my motel. He told me he had learned from a trusted source that Scotty had not had a heart problem. In fact, he had recently had a physical and was as fit as could be. Anthony also reported that Chloe had no significant other at the moment and she lived alone. I thanked Anthony sincerely for what he had done, but then told him it might be best if we not communicate again. I was sure he understood that I was working on something and did not want to incriminate him accidently. His parting comment was, "If you ever need a place to hang out, we have an empty bunkhouse out back.

~ ~ ~

From Boston to Jacksonville, the featureless nature of I-95 requires little of a driver and offers him few diversions. So, my mind was available and restless. As I stared out the windshield, it kept asking how I could justify running the risks involved in this operation, and in response I kept trying out different answers to the question. I must say, after all that reflection, I had absolutely no second thoughts about what I was going to do. From my perspective, Chloe was a rich psychopath who had murdered my friend – her father – and had tried to injure or perhaps kill me. I figured she had it coming.

The miles clicked by and after twenty-four hours of driving and one six hour stop in a motel I rolled into Jacksonville. There I turned in my Avis car because I was going to be in Chloe's neighborhood for the next few days and I figured a car with Florida plates would be less conspicuous than one with Massachusetts plates. Details are important.

For the same reason, I wanted to use my most effective disguise, the one with the mustache and glasses. As I was contemplating these tactical matters and walking to the Hertz office to pick up my new car, I spotted a McDonald's. It was crowded with midday customers so it seemed unlikely that anyone would pay me enough attention to notice that I had entered the men's room clean shaven and exited with a jaunty, greying mustache and a new pair of tinted glasses. By four o'clock, fortified by a cheeseburger and two coffees, I was driving south to Ocala, a different man in a new car with Florida tags and a sharp, Atlanta Braves baseball cap.

I rolled into Ocala at seven in the evening and cruised through the neighborhoods. The smell of money was everywhere. It seemed that each park and yard was manicured, and the entire town was sheltered and beautified by flamboyant tropical trees: acacia, live oaks, draped with languid Spanish moss, numerous species of palm, scarlet and yellow blooming poinsettia, schefflera, and others. Ocala was also known for the number of its thoroughbred horse farms and its most famous native son, Early Arrival, won the Triple Crown in 1974. Despite the beauty all around me, I was anxious to find my way to Chloe's house, but I forced myself to wait for darkness.

Her home was located on an enchanting street lined with date palms and festooned with crimson blooming bougainvillea. There was almost no traffic at that time of evening and there were no streetlights. The road to her house was straight, which meant I could keep an eye on comings and goings without using binoculars. Generally speaking, the location was favorable to me. My concern was that police cruisers or a private security company might regularly patrol the street. I would have to leave if they passed my parking area more than twice. After two drive-bys of her house, I headed out of town for the night. I was operating under an old principle: 'if something can go wrong, it will.'" That is why I spent the night in Gainesville, a full twenty miles north of Ocala.

At 6:15 the next morning, wearing my new disguise, I pulled into an ideal parking place. It was within sight of Chloe's house and between two cars whose owners were probably playing tennis down the hill. Twelve hours later, as the heat and humidity of central Florida began to ease slightly, Chloe appeared in her driveway, stretched briefly, and took off running down the sidewalk – directly at me. It scared the hell out of me and the only response I managed was to flip down my sun visor, which partially blocked her view of my face. Despite that, we saw each other from a distance of only six feet. I was sure she did not recognize me, though. Darkness was falling and I had on my full disguise, mustache, wig, and hat. She disappeared into the fading light and I considered making my move when she returned, but my hands were still shaking and my heart, still pounding from the shock of seeing her running right at me.

I repositioned the car and waited for her return. In the absence of streetlamps and under two enormous banyan trees, twilight quickly faded to pitch darkness. Thirty minutes later, Chloe reappeared running strongly up the hill towards her home. I watched her carefully with the binoculars as she bounced up the stairs and pulled open her front door. Her family had never locked either the ranch house or their town home. I was happy to see Chloe had brought that custom with her to her new house.

Hanging around until she returned was smart. I knew that most serious runners – and Chloe was one – adhere faithfully to their routines. I was so sure Chloe would run for about thirty minutes the next day starting around sunset that I took the day off. This not only reduced the time I was exposed on her street, but also allowed me to sleep late, go over what I was going to say to her one last time, and make sure my small satchel had the crucial items I would need when I entered the house. I had a leisurely lunch, took a nap and a shower and began my vigil at five o'clock in the evening.

Chloe left her house in her running togs at 6:35. At 6:40, after pulling on a pair of surgical gloves, I entered the house by a back door. Assuming Chloe would enter the house using the same door she used when she left, I studied the entry area to figure how I could best use the element of surprise to subdue her quickly and quietly. After looking around the basement, I decided a small utility room would be the best place to take her because there was no window or door leading to the outside. I went to the kitchen next, pulled a left-handed cotton glove from my satchel and slid it over the surgical glove on my left hand. Lastly, I took from my satchel a squirt gun,

17

pointed it at the kitchen sink and pulled the trigger. It worked perfectly. After washing the sink, there was nothing to do but wait. Squirt gun in hand, I stood on the other side of the living room from the large bay window and waited to see my old girlfriend walk across her front lawn, up the steps and into my arms. My heart was pounding.

Just as Chloe opened her front door, I pumped the last squirt of chloroform into the cotton glove on my left hand. She probably never smelled its sweet scent. As she took her second step beyond me, I slammed into her from behind, wrapping my right arm around both her arms at elbow-level and locking the chloroform-soaked glove over her nose and mouth. I drove her hard into the living room carpet and felt her struggle with great strength to throw me off her back. But she fought only briefly. I felt the tension drain from her muscles before she went limp. I pulled a roll of duct tape out of my satchel and took several wraps around her ankles, added a few more around her wrists, and finally I secured several big strips over her mouth. Convinced she would be going nowhere and making no noise, I put each article back in the satchel: tape, squirt gun, and cotton glove. I kept my surgical gloves on but removed my wig, mustache, and glasses and placed them in the satchel too. I wanted her to see me. I was not sure how the chloroform would affect her mind and it certainly would not do to have her think she had been hallucinating. Two minutes had passed, and she was beginning to regain her senses. This relieved me. Had she remained unconscious for five minutes or more she could have suffered lasting brain damage from the chloroform. I picked her up, carried her downstairs and into the utility room. There I sat her upright on the sofa.

When she first opened her eyes, they did not focus. She was half-conscious; she shook her feet, arms and legs, and a muffled sound found its way through the tape. Then her eyes widened in terror and she shook even harder. I placed my hand on her shoulder and said, "Relax, I promise I am not going to hurt you." I gave her a few seconds to process this information and continued. "Do you know who I am?"

Chloe nodded. "Is my name Frank?" She shook her head, keeping her frightened eyes on me. "Is it Remington?" She shook her head again. "Is it Sandor?" A nod. I held my hands in front of her. "Nod your head one time for each finger you see. She nodded seven times. "Good," I said. "Now, listen carefully. I want to repeat: I am not going to hurt you. If you cooperate, this will be over in fifteen minutes. Do you understand?" Nod.

She sat bolt upright, all senses working. I could tell. I pulled up a folding chair and sat leaning forward looking directly at her. "The grand jury is going to consider your case soon," I began, "but they don't hold the keys to your future. I do. Let me explain. District Attorney Andrew Snyder isn't a big fan of Scotty. The other day in private he said, 'Leave Scotty alone. He's finally quiet and I'd like him to stay that way.' Also, Snyder's new to the job and probably doesn't want to start off with such a controversial case. So, I'm quite sure that if a grand jury voted tomorrow, you would not be indicted."

"But, Chloe, I know you killed your father, just like you almost killed me back in high school. I know your relationship with him was a disaster and I know you goaded him into racing you on horseback the morning he died. I'm also pretty sure the rumors about his heart were not true. Is that right?" Chloe nodded and I silently thanked Anthony. Admitting the rumors were false was close to admitting she killed him. I pushed on. "Did you have something special planned for that ride? Yes, of course you did. You had everything arranged to make your murder plan look like a lovely morning ride. Your friend Gladys was with you so she could testify about how helpful and solicitous you were with your father all morning, but she knew nothing of the killing moment, did she? She did not see Lucky's crazed bucking and spinning, or Scotty's violent, awkward death because she had been left in the dust when the race started, right?

"So, the question is: how did you make Lucky buck him off remotely? I bet you asked someone. I know I did. I called the Hot Shot prod factory in Lincoln, Nebraska, and asked if they had such a thing as a remote-control prod. The man said, 'We don't sell 'em, but you can make 'em in about ten minutes. Just buy you a remote-control garage door opener and take out the starter button, the antenna, and the switch. Solder two wires from the business end of the prod to two flat pieces of metal and tape those metal plates to the rump of the cattle that don't move fast enough. That'll speed 'em up all right.'" I stopped talking like the man at the factory at that point because I wanted Chloe to remember everything I said. The more she remembered, the more likely she was to do what I wanted her to do.

I waited, then changed back to myself. "All you had to do, Chloe, was hide the prod, which is the size of a pen, and the receiver and switch, each the size of a pack of cigarettes, in Lucky's saddlebag and place the metal pieces so they lay flat against the horse when you tied the saddlebag down. When the race started you waited until Gladys had fallen way behind and you and Scotty were galloping at full speed. Then you pushed the button and WHAM, 4500 volts hit your father's horse in the rump! That's a lot of juice, man. Not enough to kill the horse, but it would certainly make her buck like the baddest goddamned bronco in Florida as long as you held that button down. Your poor dad flew off that horse, did a half-flip and landed on his head. It snapped his neck and killed him instantly. And that's what's called cold-blooded, premeditated patricide."

After the 'accident,' you just took the parts out of the saddlebag quick and easy and stashed them away until you were safe and alone and could dispose of them permanently." I stopped my monologue and looked at Chloe. Her eyes were cast downward.

"Do I have your attention now?" I asked Chloe. She looked up but did not nod this time. "Well, if I have *your* attention, imagine how interested the DA would be if he were here.

"Was that pretty close to how it happened?" I asked. "If so, there might be a small patch or two of burnt hair or a bald spot where the voltage entered Lucky's body. The genius in this story is, even if I've got some of its elements wrong, it's so feasible that any grand jury would want to indict you. And if they found you guilty of murder, they'd still be doing the right thing, they'd just be doing it for the wrong reasons. And the last fun part is, Florida uses the electric chair. How ironic!

"It's a strong case, no doubt, but your greed makes indictment a certainty. You had a twenty-million-dollar windfall waiting for you when Scotty died, but you had to have it right away and were willing to kill your own father to get your hands on it.

"Chloe, are you listening to me?" Again, she nodded. I have put everything I have just told you, and more, on paper. All of it is in this manila envelope which will be delivered to DA Snyder on Wednesday morning, but you have the power to stop that from happening. Do you want to know how?" Another nod.

I laid a deposit slip from my Cayman bank on the table next to her and said, "By depositing one million dollars into this bank account before the close of business next Tuesday. Let me stress, you must make the deposit anonymously and to the numbered account. No names are to be mentioned. I will call the bank at close of business Wednesday. If the entire million has been deposited, I will burn this envelope and say nothing more about it to anyone ever. I know you are thinking, 'He'll be back in a year asking for more.' But I won't. Part of the reason I need this money is because my mother is ill and has no insurance. I swear to you on her name that I will not ask you for money again.

"One last thing now. I want you to slide off the sofa and make your way to the stairs and then to the upper floor. I want to be sure you can make it to the kitchen counter where I left you a pair of scissors. Chloe made it easily enough up the stairs and into the kitchen. Once there, I ordered her to go back to the room and wait for thirty minutes before leaving it.

I had parked in a cull-de-sac two blocks from Chloe's house. I tried to walk casually through the very dark night with satchel in hand. I turned in my rental car at the Jacksonville airport at 9:10 and was asleep in my hotel in New York by 2:00 a.m.

EPILOGUE

Chloe deposited one million dollars in Mr. Barnett's account before the deadline I had given her. I kept my word and did not make contact with District Attorney Snyder. He followed his political instincts and saw to it that the grand jury did not indict Chloe for the death of her father.

After helping my mother select a new apartment, I placed my money in several Caribbean banks, and moved to a small town in Panama under another assumed name. I lived a comfortable but solitary life there with seven geese I kept in my fenced yard as an alarm in case of an intruder. I kept my escape plan current and never went anywhere without two handguns, one in my shoulder holster, one on my ankle. I chose the solitary life because I knew Chloe would use her money to look for me and to take me down if she found me. After eighteen months in Panama, I moved to a gated community on Grand Cayman Island.

Although I planned to stay there forever, I began to miss home. I had enjoyed week after week, month after month of perfect sun, sand, and the turquoise sea, but I dreamed of Boston delis, fall football, a couple of friends, and my mother, whom I had not seen in over five years. So, I returned to the States and rented a small house on the grounds of an estate in Newport, Rhode Island. It met my needs perfectly. I received my mail at the owners' address. I parked my car in a shed behind the house, and I even put up a fence and bought seven new geese.

On the morning of my forty-fourth birthday, I awoke with a pounding headache. I rolled out of bed and stumbled into the bathroom to find some aspirin. There I was greeted by seven headless geese and a note written on the mirror that said,

Happy Birthday
B seein U

A LONG SHOT

It is a perfect day for mourning. A man in a black suit and black hat opens his car door, plants his feet on soggy ground, and slowly unfolds his six-foot six-inch frame. Tattered clouds in a sullen sky run before a stiff Atlantic breeze. A thunder shower, dying but not yet dead, sends its last icy pellets into the drab landscape and iron-grey sea. The man walks stiffly, head down, shoulders hunched against the elements, to the end of a pathway and stops. There, across an open field, he sees it; the backboard he and his recently deceased father had fastened to that magnificent white pine on his eleventh birthday, twenty-five years ago almost to the day. Even at this distance, he can see that most of the net has rotted away and the hoop is black with rust.

He continues downhill across the wet, overgrown grass and halts about fifteen feet from the basket. It sticks out defiantly, still a regulation ten feet above the ground and ready for play. The man remains there motionless for a very long time while memories fly at him in droves, like birds winging their way across time. He considers each one as it comes to him and when at last, he turns to leave, he does not walk as if he is still mourning; his head is up, and his step is light.

~ ~ ~

I was born in Boston in 1953. At the time my father, Dmitri Gavronski, was a Soviet physicist working in Moscow. My mother, Elena Sviridovna, was teaching at a junior high school outside Boston. My parents met at the university in Moscow. He was a weight-lifting intellectual and a proud agnostic; she, a devout, but clandestine Roman Catholic. She was also a striking woman of Finnish descent, with high cheekbones, blond hair, and blue eyes. She and Dmitri managed to see each other often, despite their busy schedules, because being together was proof that life could be better and they needed proof. Life was hard for them, as it was for most

Soviet citizens in the early 1950's. World War II had ravaged their country and communism, the social theory that had given hope to the working class, had not only failed to deliver, it had disillusioned people and impoverished much of the population.

On a bitter February night, after the couple had eaten a supper of black bread and tea in Elena's freezing dorm room, Dmitri watched with a sense of foreboding as Elena turned on her portable radio, and turned up the volume to cover what she was about to say. She had been preoccupied lately. Dmitri knew he was about to learn why.

"I love you, Dima," she said in a shaky voice. "Please believe me. But I have a chance to leave this godless disaster of a country and I am going to do it or die trying."

Trembling from the cold and the adrenaline coursing through his body, Dmitri managed to say, "God, you are the most wonderful woman but, Lena, this is so dangerous. If you're caught ... you could end up dying in a Siberian jail."

"I'm at peace with my decision. God will be with me."

Dmitri moved closer to her and whispered in her ear, "Make your crossing as far north as possible. The border guards will be less vigilant the farther north you go." He put his arms around her, and they held each other. "I will find a way to follow you. Wait and see."

"I will wait," she said.

Dmitri learned of my birth through Elena's brother who discreetly slipped him a photo of me. On the back of it was written 'Alexei 31.10.53'. For security reasons he did not carry that photo with him in the USSR, but he did when he reached the West. I found it in his wallet after his death.

Dmitri was in awe of Elena then and remained so throughout his life. That is why, shortly after her death, he set about writing her biography. He worked on it desperately until he realized he was not up to the task. He was a physicist, not a biographer. So, he said to me over dinner one night, "Let's collaborate on it, son. It'll be fun." I agreed immediately and never regretted it. During our five-year partnership I learned far more about my parents and their love affair and struggles than appear in the book.

24

For nine years after Elena's departure, Dmitri suppressed his dreams of a life of freedom in the West with his wife and son. Instead, he devoted all his energy to impressing his superiors with his commitment to communism and the Soviet government. During those years he proved himself a capable physicist, a talented bureaucrat, and an avid communist. In recognition of his dedication, he was promoted to Deputy Director of the State Physics Lab in Moscow. At that bureaucratic level, he knew he would occasionally receive invitations to physics gatherings abroad. A symposium in New York was the first one he saw that met his needs. Asking no one's permission and approving his own paperwork, he boarded his Aeroflot flight that fateful day with great trepidation, fearing that security thugs were aboard and waiting to arrest him. During the long walk from his gate to the Customs Terminal, Dmitri's heart beat so hard he swore he could see it pounding through his shirt. Finally, he spotted a Custom's official walking towards him. With passport in hand, he stopped the official and said the words he had rehearsed endlessly: "Please take me to a safe place. I am a Soviet physicist and request political asylum." Several weeks later he was granted defector status and agreed to be debriefed by the U.S. government for six months on the world of Soviet physics. In return, the government bought him a small house and found him a job in Bell Labs' Boston campus working on non-classified uses for semi-conductors and silicon lasers.

The odds makers who made book on the Celtics and Red Sox would have called my parents' union a long shot, but in the late summer of 1963 they married in Waban, Massachusetts. I was their Best Man.

~ ~ ~

The U.S. government and Dmitri were close to finishing his debriefing when our life began to change. Elena was downtown on a beautiful fall afternoon when she became aware that the sunlight had dimmed. Her first thought was: *it is probably an airplane making its final approach into Logan.* But she heard no jet engines roaring overhead. She stopped on the busy sidewalk to take stock. Women in high heels clicked by. Traffic was moving normally. Then the

25

shadow disappeared, and Elena resumed her walk, but she felt uneasy. *Is something wrong with me? My eyes? My head ...* and then it happened. It was as if a hundred photographers were standing in front of her taking pictures with high powered blue flashbulbs. At first, she saw only a shimmering light blue, but gradually the blue darkened until soon she was engulfed in blackness.

In the ambulance, she reached out to hold Dmitri's hand and felt it close around hers. As they raced through the city, her sight started to return. First, a midnight blue, then a lighter blue with outlines of her surroundings. Within ten minutes she could see again. In relief, she squeezed Dmitri's hand but as she looked up to smile at him, she saw that she was holding the hand of the ambulance nurse. He relinquished her hand, smiled and said, "It was nice while it lasted."

Seeing again almost brought her to tears, but she believed crying was a sign of weakness, a first step on the road to surrender. So, she focused on me, her ten-year-old son, her primary responsibility in this world, and on Jesus who, she believed, would help manage this crisis. This reaction was typical of Elena: she willfully wrested control of her emotions from the frightened, young woman she would not allow herself to be.

Dmitri arrived in time to hear the ER doctor tell Elena that he found both eyes normal. Pulling a prescription pad from his pocket, the young man explained he was writing down the name and phone number of a neuro-ophthalmologist in town, one Hyman Zimmerman. He described him as a wonderful human being and renowned in his field and he urged Elena to make an appointment with him soon. "He may well be able to detect something we did not," the young doctor said.

"I understand," Elena replied. Life in the Soviet Union had taught her to know when to pick up on the implication of a remark, rather than interpret it literally. In this case, she took the doctor's comment to mean: we could not do for you what we should have done, and your symptoms require a better work-up. "Help me remember that," she said to Dmitri, who nodded. He had read the same meaning into the doctor's remarks.

Having been given a light sedative, Elena drifted in and out of sleep while they waited for their discharge papers. Twice, while only partially awake, she said, "I don't want Alex or his school grades to suffer because he is worried about me. So, please, Dima, not a word about this to him. Okay?"

Elena put off seeing Dr. Zimmerman for six weeks. She had good excuses: Dmitri was starting a new job, I was going to a new school, and she had just been appointed the high school's first guidance counselor. But the real reason was fear. She needed time to prepare herself for the answer she expected from Dr. Zimmerman.

During those six weeks, I became aware that something was amiss. The first hint was that my mother started smoking – secretively. One night, while looking out my bedroom window, I saw her pacing up and down our driveway. When she stopped and lit a cigarette, I could not believe my eyes. Shortly thereafter, Dmitri came out and they argued. They spoke in Russian and I could not hear them well, but I understood the gist of their disagreement.

Also, around that time, my father began cleaning up the kitchen after dinner. In his culture, this act would have been revolutionary. My father's contemporaries felt it was demeaning for them, the men of their households, to do kitchen work, but my father did it night after night while she sat at the kitchen table and talked with him or worked on school papers.

Dmitri was not a revolutionary, but his presence in our household was upsetting me. During his first week in our new house, he sat me down on the sofa and said, "I would like you to call me father or dad, Alexei. Could you do that even though I don't seem like your dad yet?"

I looked right at him and said loudly, "No, I can't!" after which I jumped off the sofa and ran to my room. I was reeling from the news just delivered that Dmitri was going to live with us permanently. For some time, I objected to everything he did. If he asked me to take out the garbage, I told him I had to finish my homework. When he heard the Good Humor man's

27

bell and offered to treat me to ice cream, I would say, "no, thanks" and ask Elena sitting right next to him for ice cream money. When he tried to teach me card games, I was disinterested, and when he tried to learn about American customs and sports from me, I told him it was too complicated to explain.

At school, his presence had an immediate effect on my grades: disciplinary incidents up, academic grades down. This really bothered Elena who took out her worries on Dmitri. Despite my orneriness, he played his cards well, especially for a person inexperienced with children. One evening he said, "How about a bedtime story? I tell good ones." I probably just grunted. But he earned a few kopeks with me that night for telling a great story about a bank robber who had invented a paint that made him invisible. To his credit, he was attempting to bring some normalcy to our house, but normal for us had changed forever.

Dmitri worked long hours at his new job because he had much to learn and was conscientious. I was glad he worked so hard because it gave me more time alone with my mother. I was a mama's boy, I know. I adored her, although she was not the lovey-dovey type. Life had dealt Elena many harsh hands, the most horrific of which was to live through the Siege of Leningrad as a teenager. This Nazi holocaust lasted from September 1941 to January 1944 and took the lives of a million civilian residents of that city, including Elena's mother. Later in life, while attempting to flee to the West from the USSR, she faced the possibility of freezing to death and losing her unborn child. Abandoned by her so-called guide, Elena did not panic nor surrender the idea of reaching the border. She simply grew even more determined to succeed. Luck and clear thinking enabled her to steal a truck and drive through the night to Storskog, Norway, a border crossing point 400 kilometers north of the Arctic Circle. But Elena was proudest of the outcome of her third life and death struggle. That struggle involved a decade's worth of uncertainty, doubt, loneliness, and food stamps that came with raising a child as single parent in a foreign country.

I asked Dmitri several times over the years where my

mother's determination came from and each time he answered similarly: "It's a quality some Finns have," he said. "They even have a word for it: *sisu*. It means - when things get tough, people like your mom get tougher."

She used to tell me: "Ten percent of life is what happens to you. Ninety percent is how you react to it."

To be sure she favored determination and persistence over hugs and kisses, but she loved tucking me in every night and saying, "Sleep tight. Don't let the bedbugs bite." And she loved hearing me reply, "I love you one hundred," because she knew that was an enormous number to me and that I really did love her that much.

My parents were happy to be moving to the house the government had purchased for Dmitri, but I was not because it meant I would have to go to a new school. I do not know how it happened, but somehow, before the end of my first day there, my nickname had become 'the Russian.' This infuriated me and got me off to a poor start, to say the least. I was only ten, but I knew Russia was our enemy. The previous year we had almost gone to war with them for putting their rockets in Cuba. For a week or so I went after anyone who called me by that name. One day I was in four fights, but I was big for my age so I won all the fights.

I hated my heritage, and yet I could not deny it. My name, Alexei Dmitriovich Gavronski, was pure Russian and I hated the way it sounded when spoken by a native Russian speaker. On the plus side, I was born in America and I had a U.S. passport.

I thought about these facts and arguments all the time but could not package them in a way that would make me the all-American boy I wanted to be. In the end, I had to face the fact that I was either both American and Russian, or neither. That was not who I wanted to be, but it was who I was.

That night, while unpacking in his bedroom, Dmitri overheard me talking to my mother about my new nickname. Dmitri was 6'1," but he looked shorter because he was so broad. He had a close cropped, thick black beard and a receding hairline. He had been a weightlifter in his twenties and looked like he could still lift the back end of any car over his head. He had wandered across the hall to my bedroom while I was talking and suddenly filled the doorframe of my room. He was wearing only a pair of red briefs. I was surprised he had copious black hair on his chest and back too. "That is totally incorrect about your new nickname," he shouted. It was the first time I had heard him raise his voice. "I'll go to school with you tomorrow and stop that forever."

"Good," I said. "And go like you're dressed right now. That way Mrs. Zapp, my principal, will pay more attention to you." Dmitri looked down at himself, then at Elena. There was a moment of silence. Then they started to giggle. Before long, they were both laughing. When Elena tucked me in that night, I made sure she knew I did not want my parents coming to school to fight my battles. Before falling asleep, it occurred to me how quickly and absolutely Dmitri had taken my side. *Maybe that's what fathers do*, I thought.

Many years later, Dmitri told me that he laid in bed during those first weeks in the new house trying to figure out what else we might have in common until he realized there was a better way to solve the problem: *I will become interested in Alex's interests and not just superficially, but I will develop real, deeply down interests.* Having found a solution to his problem, he applied it: he bought two tickets to a basketball game between the Wellesley Firehouse and the Waban High School teachers. It was a fund-raiser in which Bob Cousy, the Boston Celtics' captain, was going to play. He was my idol. I thought everything about Cousy was cool, from his nickname, the Cooz, to his cat-like quickness and command of his team on court. Riding the MTA to the game a week later, Dmitri asked me one question after another about basketball and the Celtics and he became a Cousy-Celtics fan before we found our seats. That night, Cousy kept the Teachers in the lead with his incredible passes. Any time a Teacher found himself open near the basket; he found the ball flying right at him. I talked about Cousy all way home, so much that I forgot to thank Dmitri, and I did not fall asleep until 3 a.m.

Dmitri was so pleased that he awoke Elena to tell her. "I think him and me are going to make it after all," he concluded.

Elena smiled at the confused expression on his face as he forgot his grammar rules and mangled his usage of those pronouns. Then she started to laugh. She laughed until she cried. Dmitri sat on her bedside and stroked her hair.

It was a shame Dmitri and I could not have kept our peace momentum going, but just as it looked as if we had found common ground, we hit a snag. It happened on a Saturday morning. I hopped on my bike and rode three miles to the nearest basketball court. The morning was damp and cold, typical of fall in Boston, but I thought nothing of it. I practiced for about an hour in a cold drizzle and pedaled home with my flimsy Celtics t-shirt sticking to my skin.

I ate some cereal and was headed upstairs to take a hot shower when I noticed a note on the counter:

"A, have gone for errand. Will call. D"

The note struck me as odd, but I forgot about it immediately because I was absorbed in a Hardy Boys mystery. I ate and read for half an hour, made a sandwich, and climbed back in bed to read some more, but could not concentrate. I always worried when my mother was late. *If she'd just call,* I thought. Minutes later, the phone rang, and Dmitri said, "Just wanted to say all's well, Alex. We're at church and we'll be home soon." I was so relieved I said only, "K bye," and hung up. Then I said a short prayer thanking God for keeping her – and him – safe.

I heard the truck come down the driveway but did not rush downstairs to say hello. I was hurt and peeved. Elena had been gone three hours without telling me she was going out, and when I walked into the kitchen twenty minutes after their return, Dmitri didn't say hello, but rather, "Quiet, your mother is sleeping."

"Now? How come?"

"Well, she felt a little dizzy at church and thought it was extra glass of wine she drank last night. So, she called and asked me to pick her up," Dmitri said. "Not the big deal." But Dmitri did not look at me as he spoke, and his words clashed with reality. *If he had gone the three miles to church to fetch Elena, where had he been for the past three hours? And why did his note say he would call? About what?* I felt like the

31

television lawyer Perry Mason picking apart a defendant's story, waiting for a better explanation. When none was forthcoming, I headed for the backdoor. As I reached for the doorknob, I turned and heard myself say, "What really happened?"

It was an awful moment. I thought my father was going to say, *'Are you calling me a liar?'* His duplicity and my resentment were about to boil over into angry words. I could have played the little boy and started to cry. He could have pulled the paternal card and sent me to my room. But we both exercised restraint. I know now that his primary concern was not with me or my accusation. It was with Elena and how he would deal with her anger if he told the truth? He had only a second to decide. Just as I turned to leave, Dmitri said, "She had a seizure."

"What's that?"

"It's when your brain doesn't work right for a minute or two. It caused your mother to lose her consciousness, which is common with the seizures. After she woke up, someone drove her to ER and called me."

"And what did they say at the hospital?"

"The doctor said he hadn't determined what caused your mother's seizure, but he wants more tests on Monday. He gave her some medicine that will let her sleep for several hours." Without a word, I turned and started to leave. "Alex," Dmitri said sharply, "Your mother doesn't want to worry you. That's why she didn't want to tell you about her seizure." I bent down, picked up the basketball, and walked out into the cold, damp afternoon.

I was going to pedal back to the playground, but it was too far. So, I walked down to the end of our backyard and slumped down on an old bench there. Just sitting by myself helped calm my nerves and clarify my thinking. I did sense that Dmitri was genuinely worried about Elena. At least we had that in common. And his second story rang true. He probably did want to tell me what had happened, but something had stopped him.

He said to me once, "Always tell the truth. It'll keep you out of trouble." But when he confronted his personal moment of truth, he betrayed his belief and rejected his own advice.

~ ~ ~

Thinking about her seizure made me wonder if God were concerned about Elena. He had made life difficult for her so far. She seemed a little like the lost sheep we discussed in Sunday school after reading Luke 15, verses 4-6:

What man of you, having a hundred sheep,

If he lose one of them, doth not leave the ninety-nine in the wilderness

And go after that which is lost, until he finds it?

And when he hath found it, he layeth it on his shoulders, rejoicing.

Mr. Miller, our teacher, asked if we thought it wise to leave the flock of ninety-nine to look for one lost sheep. Dan Baggins was the first to shout out an opinion. "No! The shepherd was stupid because some wolves could eat the lambs while the shepherd was away." I took the opposing position, arguing that it was smart to go look for the lost lamb because that showed all one hundred lambs that the shepherd loved each of them and would never leave one of them to die alone. "Maybe it really means, if you are lost, God will look for you and find you," I suggested.

The proposition of risking all to save one intrigued me and while practicing free throws one day, out of the blue a question occurred to me: *Would God go looking for Elena if she were the lost sheep? She lost her mother and father in the war. So, in a way she was alone like the lost sheep in the Bible story.* As I could not answer my own question, I did what boys standing around basketball courts do: I thought, *Okay, we'll let this shot decide. If I sink it, God would go look for her. If I miss ... well, we know what that means.* I was a good free throw shooter and was confident I could make the shot, but I was a bit reckless too at that age and I missed the shot. This was upsetting because I thought God might have been sending me a message, but I still thought *God should have been looking out for Elena. She had been through so much. Instead, He had just let her have a seizure.* Regardless of what God would or would not do, I decided I would always do my best to help her.

33

~ ~ ~

A few days before Elena's first appointment with Dr. Zimmerman, Dmitri came up with a project that would get her 'boys', as she called us, out of the house and keep our imaginations occupied. He burst in the kitchen door earlier than usual on the afternoon of my eleventh birthday, gave me my first Russian bear hug – I still remember his bristly beard on my face – and shouted "*S Dnem Rozhdeniya!*" Happy Birthday. "Come out to the truck," he said. There he pointed to a gleaming white basketball backboard in the truck bed. The hoop, net, screws and bolts were on the front seat. "It shall be a big work, but on Saturday we shall begin," he bellowed.

The next afternoon, he and I ranged over our four acres and decided the best place to put it would be on the only patch that was reasonably flat. On one edge of this area, stood seven or eight ancient apple trees; on the other, a giant white pine. Its ramrod-straight trunk had been limbed by a previous owner so that its lowest branches were well above where the backboard would go.

Early Saturday morning, a truck from the lumber mill pulled into our yard and drove down to the white pine where two men unloaded lumber, tools, equipment, nails, bolts, screws, an extension ladder and more onto the dewy grass. Ten minutes later they gave us a beep and a wave and were gone. Swallowing the last of his coffee Dmitri said, "Okay, Alex, let's go onto the road with this show!" I rolled my eyes, but I was excited too and ran out the door in front of him.

Twelve-and-one-half hours later we sat down for the first time since our lunch break. "My back and neck and shoulders are so tired they can hardly hold my head on, I mean up," he said in a weak voice. "I must have hammered my poor left thumb seven thousand times, and my calves and feet are on fire from standing for hours on those ladder rugs. Why do they call them rugs, anyway?" I was so tired I could not answer him and fell asleep as we sat. I remember dreaming that my father was calling me, and he was, but I could not answer. I had measured, sawed, glued, and hammered until every 2 x 6 and 2 x 4 was snug and secure in its place. I had drilled holes and tightened bolts. I had hauled the backboard and each piece of its support structure aloft where my father had muscled each part into position. I had learned how to use a miter box to cut angles and a moveable pulley to lift things that were too heavy for me to lift alone. "It's pure physics, Alex," Dmitri had explained proudly earlier that afternoon, "gravity, energy and force. See how good it works!"

"Look what we did," Dmitri said, jostling me gently. The backboard was reflecting the moon light. I opened my eyes to see its pristine white surface shining down upon us in the cold, dark evening like a rectangular harvest moon. Below, the black, arthritic branches of the old apple trees reached up to it as if in supplication. The hoop, decorated with a Kelly green and white Celtics net, stuck out confidently, precisely ten feet above the ground, ready to signal the success or failure of every shot aimed at it.

"Don't move any muscles," Dmitri said as he limped to a duffel bag in the apple orchard and withdrew a new basketball. "Now is inauguration. Take first shot." I took careful aim and pushed the ball up with both hands. It arced into the night, fell back towards earth, hit the rim, circled it once, and fell out.

"I am too tired," I said.

"I know. That one we don't count." Dmitri put his hand on my shoulder and kept it there as we walked home.

~ ~ ~

Building and having my own backboard was so exciting that for several days I did not think much about Elena's seizure. Part of my mind was working to hide the truth from me, as my parents were, and part wanted to know the truth. I had been sleeping fitfully and waking up before sunrise almost every morning. When I could not go back to sleep, I would prop my head on my hand, and stare out the window at the delicate branches silhouetted against the pearlescent sky. As I focused on designs the branches made, I sometimes saw caricatures of faces – some familiar, others not – but the most memorable face to appear was my mother's. She was in profile, looking sad, and smoking a cigarette. Then, the wind blew, the branches shifted, and she was gone.

The morning after our great construction project I did not

35

wake up with the sun or with the alarm. I even slept through Sunday school. "How come you didn't wake me up?" I asked Dmitri as I came downstairs.

"Relax, my boy," he said. "The life is a short one. Your mother and I agreed that you worked so hard yesterday you deserve a day of rest today." I was elated and turned around on the stairs, ran to my room, and pulled on some clothes.

I tucked the new basketball under my arm and shouted to Dmitri as I ran out. "You know where I'll be."

My first practice session on my home court was dreamlike. A heavy ground fog softened all sharp edges and angles and tampered with my depth perception. I made three shots in a row from the top of the key but could not sink even one from four steps to the left. Our backboard was strong and true, though, and I was thrilled.

~ ~ ~

Although I knew nothing of my parents' impending meeting with Dr. Zimmerman, I awoke twice during the night and noticed their bedroom light was on. I awoke again just before sunrise to watch the morning light lift the darkness and to listen for a while to a woodpecker's staccato rhythm echo through the woods.

At the dinner table that evening, I learned that Dmitri and Elena had been talking about me with Dr. Zimmerman, while I had been talking about them with God. I had asked: *God, if I work really hard and learn how to make some really difficult shots, would You make my mother better? Everybody asks You for help. Why shouldn't I? Especially since this is not a selfish request. I would be asking that You help someone else, not me.* So, I made my proposal. *God, let's say if I make three out of five from the foul line, then could You guarantee that Elena and her new doctor will like each other? I'm afraid that if she doesn't like him, she won't do what he says and won't get better.* Having drawn up the terms of the agreement, I now had to execute it and to my relief and delight, I made three out of five. I jogged back to the house proud of my afternoon's work.

While I was lining up God's support with my good shooting, Dmitri and Elena were in Dr. Zimmerman's office.

He had impressed them both and they wanted to tell me everything. So we sat in the kitchen and they talked. Uncharacteristically, Elena was full of praise. "We were sitting in the waiting room and your father was holding my hand because I was so nervous when out walks this cute little man wearing a yellow bow tie and a suit – no white coat. He had frizzy hair and a carefully trimmed greying mustache". She went on and on. "He's an old-fashioned gentleman," she said. "I mean he's courtly. He even bowed slightly when he approached us and said in a gravelly voice, 'Good morning, I am Hy Zimmerman. Most of my patients call me Dr. Z.' He shook Dmitri's hand," Elena continued, "then he placed my hand on his forearm and escorted me to his office as if we were going to a cotillion." Dmitri chuckled and added that for ten minutes they chatted amicably about their lives and families, but he knew Dr. Z was working because the Gavronskis were doing most of the talking. Dmitri looked at me and said, "When your mother mentioned that you were not yet aware of her illness, Dr. Z became very serious."

"What illness?" I asked.

"I took some notes while he was talking," Dmitri said pulling a piece of paper from his pocket. "Let me see. He said he was sure you already suspected that something was wrong at home and you probably felt your parents were hiding something from you. Was he right?"

"Yep, I did. What illness?"

Elena studied my eyes while holding my hands. I waited. "Alex, I must tell you that last fall I lost my sight in both eyes for about ten minutes. You can't imagine how scary it was for me and I didn't want to scare you too. That's why I didn't tell you." I could tell how nervous she was from her jittery voice. "Dr. Z said we should not keep this secret from you, and we won't from now on. Your dad and I will keep you up to date, okay?"

I smiled and said, "Okay, Mom," but I was not entirely happy about their decision. It sounded like something I'd rather forget, but I knew I couldn't.

Having addressed this issue, Dr. Z did a neurological exam, ordered three basic blood tests, and put Elena on corticosteroids. "Now we wait to see the results of these three blood tests and if the medicine helps," he said. Dr. Z bade them a warm goodbye saying, "if you develop a new symptom or concern, call me and I will see you that same day or the next day. And, please, tell Alex he's welcome to come to your next appointment if he wishes."

On the way home, Dmitri described Dr. Z as "intimidatingly intelligent" and Elena thanked God for bringing Dr. Z to her.

~ ~ ~

Early one morning the following week, Dmitri saw me staring out my bedroom window.

"What is up?" he said

"Nothin'."

"Why not?" Dmitri asked, taking a seat on the edge of the bed. "Is everything okay?"

"How come you don't believe in Heaven?" I asked.

"Wow! What a question for six o'clock in the morning." He waited, hoping for a reprieve, but I wanted an answer. I just waited. "Well, I don't believe in Heaven because I cannot see it or touch it. I don't know where it is, and I don't know anyone who has been there. In science we have a method for testing ideas and proving or disproving them, but I can't test Heaven."

"But Mom believes in it," I said.

"Yes, she does. So, we have difference of opinion. There's nothing wrong with that. And what do you believe? Have you made up your mind yet?"

"I would like there to be a Heaven, but I don't know if there is one."

"Fair enough. Then the question is, do you want to go make pancakes?"

"Yeah!" I said, jumping out of bed.

Elena had suggested that Dmitri think of being with me as play time, not problem-solving time. The pancake come-on worked well. Over the years we ate many pancakes together.

My parents went to the hospital Monday morning to have blood drawn for the three tests Dr. Z had ordered. Rather than stay home alone, I went to school early and worked on that difficult shot from the left side of the key. I needed to be able to make that shot. Otherwise, an imaginary Cousy might decide it was my weak spot, and take advantage of me some day in a game of H-O-R-S-E.

While shooting around, I said a little prayer thanking God for bringing Elena and Dr. Z together without suggesting that my three out of five shooting had contributed to their meeting. Of course, I did not *know* that my shots had helped, but it was very coincidental if they had not. So, I tried my luck again. *God, if I sink six shots in a row, will You let my Mother come home this afternoon with good scores on her tests?* I assumed God would figure this was a good bet for Him. After all, how many kids are going to make six shots in a row? But I chose the easiest shot there is. I stood two feet to the right of the basket and banked the ball off the backboard and through the hoop, six for six. It was so easy, I wondered if God felt tricked. *Not possible! There is no little boy in the world who can trick God,* I reassured myself. Dr. Z called three days later to tell Elena the results of all the tests were normal. "How have you been feeling?" he asked.

"Quite well," Elena answered, "and I have been working full time."

"In that case, I'll see you in a month."

~ ~ ~

Time passed quickly that winter as each of us was fully engaged in his work. Dmitri, happy to be in America, was assimilating well under *The New York Times'* tutelage. The newspaper kept him current and improved his English, except for his legendary misuse of colloquialisms. (Some who knew him well were convinced that Dmitri cultivated this 'defect' for fun.)

The assassination of President John Kennedy occurred on 22 November 1963. Dmitri watched in awe and disbelief as live, uncensored reports went out to the world chronicling America's shame. He was so impressed by the openness with which it was handled that he vowed to become a U.S. citizen. It took time, but he and Elena fulfilled that goal.

At the beginning of the school year, Elena was named her high school's first guidance counselor, a position she had unofficially created and developed over the past five years. The appointment was her community's acknowledgement of her foresight and leadership, and it gave her a morale boost.

I worked and fought my way through the winter months at school but played little basketball because of the weather. The layoff was good for me though. When spring arrived, I felt rejuvenated and excited about returning to my private court and honing my skills.

In early summer, just as my mother's senior students were about to graduate, Elena thought she might be coming down with the flu. Her shoulders, arms, and neck were achy and stiff. When she mentioned these symptoms to Dr. Z, he said, "The time has come to biopsy your temporal arteries. They can inform us if the passage of blood to the eyes is normal. The procedure is simple, lasts 30 minutes at most, is low risk, and you will feel fine tomorrow. How soon would you like to do this?"

"As soon as possible," Elena said without hesitation.

Throughout the spring I practiced the shot that had defied me. I had not mastered it, but I was no longer intimidated by it. I decided that when or if the time came for a showdown, I would go to the one-handed push shot and I would take it from four steps left of center at the top of the key. It was a 23-foot shot, which would require skill and nerve to make under duress. But I would be asking God for a great deal, so I had to give him my best in return.

As soon as Elena came home from her appointment, she told me the biopsy had been scheduled for Thursday, two days hence. I knew what a biopsy entailed. Dmitri had explained it to me. But when I imagined a doctor cutting into my mother's head, I saw blood and felt pain. My imagination actually made me nauseated. I stayed with her until Dmitri came home from work, but then I grabbed the ball and headed down to the court. The light that early summer evening seemed gilded and enhanced the colors of the young spring grass. The soft air was filled with the sweet aromas of cut grass, and the flower blossoms miraculously appearing on our ancient apple trees. I sat on the bench, retied my sneakers, and said out loud, "*God, I'm back. Thanks for my mother's test results last winter, and I hope You'll help me today because she has a very important test to take.* I paused for a few seconds before making my final commitment. *I've been practicing really hard. So, if you agree, I'm ready to go. If I make the shot, you'll let my mother see again for life, right? That's the deal, okay? If I miss, you do whatever you want."*

My heart was pounding as I walked to the top of the key. *Did I really say, "You do whatever you want"? This one shot could affect the rest of my mother's life. It was real-life, big-time risk-taking.* For a moment, I thought of that Biblical shepherd, but by the time I took my four steps to the left, I was thinking only about the shot.

I squared my shoulders to the basket and planted my feet for balance, right foot slightly in front of the left. I focused on a point at the back of the hoop, kept my right elbow close to my body and placed my left hand on the front of the ball, locking it against my shooting hand. I took a deep breath, exhaled, and shot. My right arm flew up and my left hand fell away, leaving the ball balanced on my fingertips. As my arm reached its full extension, I snapped my wrist, launching the ball on its flight. It felt like it had too much backspin. So, when it hit the front of the rim, it popped straight up, then fell straight down through the green and white cords. I dropped to my knees and raised both hands and my face to the Heavens.

I desperately wanted someone to celebrate with but there was no one, no one I could explain this to, no one who could understand how much I had been through and how much it meant.

~ ~ ~

In his office, after the procedure, Dr. Z handed Elena a form to sign. He noted how she turned her head to favor her better eye while reading the paper and said, "You can't see well from that left eye, can you, my dear?"

"And I can't fool you for five seconds, can I?" Elena answered. "Do you think I am going to lose my sight permanently?"

"The state of the arteries reveal that you have suffered two strokes, one at the back of each eye. Only time will tell, Elena, whether you will lose your vision or not."

"Be honest, now. I'm strong. I would rather know so I can be prepared. I want your opinion."

"A person who has had one stroke is at greater risk to have another than a person who has never had a stroke. The odds are, if you live to be seventy or older, that you might lose vision at least in one eye. I'm very sorry to tell you that, Elena, but remember, medicine is both a science and an art. Statistics is one thing, attitude is another. You are one determined woman. I would not be at all surprised if you beat the odds."

I was waiting for them in the kitchen when they arrived. They looked somber. Before I could speak, Dmitri said, "Okay, Alex, I will give it to you with a nutshell." Neither Elena nor I offered a correction. He moved close to me at the kitchen table and looked straight at me. "Dr. Zimmerman removed pieces of two arteries with no problem and looked at them under his microscope. Based on what he saw, he told us that last year strokes stopped the flow of blood to your mom's eyes for a few seconds. That's why she briefly lost her vision and has had headaches ever since." Speaking slowly and quietly, Dmitri explained that the medicine Dr. Z gave her was meant to allow more blood to flow through those arteries. "He says the medicine is the best they have, but it is new so he cannot predict how well it will work. We just have to hope for the best."

Dmitri tried to finesse the subject of blindness by mentioning how kind Dr. Z had been. But when he paused, I asked, "Are you going to be blind, Mom?"

"Only time will tell, my sweet boy," she said, "but it is a possibility." With those words, I sank to the floor. I had been leaning against the sink when suddenly my legs felt rubbery and simply would not support me. Elena and Dmitri came and sat on the floor next to me and put their arms around me. We sat there, backs against the kitchen cabinets, stunned.

"But, Mom, you do so much for everybody, and you go to church all the time. How can God do this to *you*?"

"We have to trust Him," she said.

"How can we? Would you trust someone who put my eyes out?" I asked as I climbed to my feet. "No, you'd probably kill him." My shock had turned to anger. *Less than two days ago I made that shot fair and square.*

Several minutes passed before Elena said, "I don't have to see to be happy, Alex. You are the reason I'm happy, really."

At that moment, Elena looked older than the woman who made my breakfast that morning. Her hands were clasped tightly in her lap, and her jaw was clenched, which pulled her lips to a semi-grimace. The expression on her pretty face, a mixture of embarrassment, angst, and determination, reminded me that life is 90 percent how you react to it: *this is the woman who made her way to that border crossing point 400 kilometers north of the Arctic Circle, alone, in the middle of the night, in mid-winter, while pregnant. I'm going to bet on her!*

I had no intention of playing basketball the next morning, but I brought the ball out of habit. I just wandered down the hill toward the old bench. As I sank down onto it, I looked skyward and said out loud, *Either You exist and don't like us, or You don't exist, and we just had some bad luck. Anyway, God, count me out.* Then I sat thinking, making sure what I said next was what I wanted to say. *I wanted You to exist, God. I wanted to have faith in You. That would have been nice. But if You existed, You wouldn't let this happen!* All was still, as if my pronouncement was being considered by every living thing around us. I was finished. I climbed slowly to my feet and began the long trek up the hill to the house, but then for some reason I turned back toward the backboard one last time and I shouted, *"Okay, God, I'm giving you one last chance. This shot is so hard I could never make it without Your help. So, if I make it ... well, who knows?"* I was probably thirty feet from the basket. I had barely enough strength to throw the ball that distance, but I heaved it in anger and desperation. My arm shot out like a piston. The exertion emptied my lungs and flung me forward onto the grass. I looked up and watched the ball describe a high arc in the twilight sky and drop through the hoop – nothing but net.

The tall man dressed in black glances at the sky repeatedly while walking back to his car and concludes he has no time to lose. He opens his trunk and pulls out a basketball and a pair of sneakers. A minute later, still in his dark suit, he is jogging back to the court, holding the ball firmly in one hand. He pulls up three feet behind the foul line, elevates two feet off the ground, and shoots a fade away jumper. It swishes through the few frayed cords of the net. As the ball rebounds off the pine tree, the man snatches it out of the air, pulls it close to his chest, flares his elbows, head-fakes to the left, spins to the right and sinks a left-handed hook. He plays hard until there is no longer enough light to see the basket.

In the morning, he will fly home and to his life and responsibilities. Because it seems unlikely, with both parents gone, that he will return to this revered place, he had decided to leave behind a memento of his attachment to it. For the last time he walks to that point four steps to the left of the top of the key. There he kneels and, with the help of a fallen branch, scoops out a hole in the soggy earth. To consecrate the land, he reaches up with cold, muddy hands and removes his clerical collar. He prints on it in bold letters, ALEX GAVRONSKI, PRIEST and COACH. Finally, he pulls from his breast pocket a plastic bag containing a snapshot of Dmitri, Elena, and Alex, arms around each other, grinning broadly, and standing in front of a banner which reads:

Boone High School
Men's Basketball Champs 1985

Alex places his collar and the picture in a small box, buries it, and bows his head in silent prayer.

BRODY UNBOWED

I first heard the eerie, monotone hum while doing chores aboard my sailboat *Circus* one summer afternoon in Michigan. I went topside and found the hum louder there. Then, the sunlight dimmed, returned, and dimmed again, as if we were experiencing an interplanetary short circuit. I looked to the sky for an answer and saw a black cloud about a quarter mile long. It was 500 meters off our stern and closing fast. I was soon to discover that this cloud was made up of countless flying insects the size of big mosquitoes. The Michigan locals called them 'midge flies.'

Before I could scramble below deck, the cloud was on top of me. The flies were attacking my exposed skin; the bites hurt and many started bleeding. The hum was so intense it hurt my ears. I felt flies on my lips, in my mouth and ears, and crawling down my throat. I gagged and choked and wanted to run for cover, but my eyes had involuntarily shut against those incessant insects and I could not open them. I stumbled, fell, then grabbed the starboard gunnel and lowered myself into the water. Underwater, I held my breath as long as possible. When I surfaced, the cloud looked like a grey smudge moving across a shiny blue sky.

Back on the boat I felt stunned, nauseated, and itchy. My face was painful and swelling and I was sickened by the black, sticky mess the midge fly carcasses made on my beautiful new teak deck. I found them in every nook and cranny of the boat for weeks.

The papers had been full of stories about the swarming midge flies. Most experts expected two hatchings that year, a phenomenon that last occurred eighty years ago, and they predicted that swarms of the flies would appear over and around Lake Michigan for the next two weeks. The authorities urged boaters to curtail their activities and held out little hope that the situation would improve within the next seven days. What was I going to do with my brother Brody who was at that moment traveling north by train to meet me for a week of sailing?

I met him that evening at the train station. "Hey, Big Brother! How you be?" I shouted, using our old greeting. Brody did not hug anyone, and he shook hands only reluctantly when he knew it would be hurtful not to. So, he limited his greeting to, "Hi, Blakie. Holy cow! What happened to your face?"

"I'll tell you all about it on the way to the boat." I said. "How was the trip?"

"Oh, it was good, except for one guy who was tailing me. Can't imagine who he was working for, but I let him know I was onto him and he got off an hour south. Otherwise, all was normal. Nice scenery as we moved north," he added. Brody's mild episodes of paranoia occurred most often after he had been to an action movie or was facing a change in his routine.

There was something imposing about Brody's appearance. Maybe it was his military posture that made him look like a man of means, one who might have a Mercedes and a chauffeur waiting nearby. He was six feet tall, had fine, symmetrical features and furtive eyes. He dressed in the elegant clothes our mother used to buy for him, but she had been gone a decade and Brody gave little thought to his wardrobe. His out-of-style, expensive but now threadbare clothing gave him the distinctive look of an eccentric Hollywood director gone to seed perhaps, or an exiled member of the Albanian royal family. His favorite garment was a black and red smoking jacket, which he wore everywhere.

In his childhood, Brody had been humiliated and bullied much more than most kids his age. So generally, he was suspicious of strangers and lacked confidence in himself. However, when he was comfortable in his surroundings, he could also be good company because, unlike most people, he listened well and had an excellent memory. The problem was that he also had a short attention span and was easily distracted. This made tracking a long discussion difficult for him.

Typically, one evening in the yacht club bar Brody was listening to a group of sailors discussing the midge fly situation. When there was a pause in the conversation, Brody interjected a couple of risqué rumors about the new Michigan State cheerleading squad. Even though his comments had no connection with the topic under discussion, some of the men told me later that they appreciated Brody's subtle suggestion that they find something better to discuss. He was given the benefit of the doubt often, just as he was that night. It was his presence that made some people pay attention to him and gave his comments import. Brody did not see the irony in this, but he did notice that people took him seriously when he spoke. So he always made it a point to thank them for their interest in what he called his "little theories." The magic of his charisma and quirky ways was something to behold.

During that summer of the midge fly, Brody turned sixty-eight, one year my senior. He had worked for forty-some years at menial jobs in a small town near Flint, Michigan. He had loved chatting with the waitresses over breakfast at McDonald's and tipping the dancers at Hooters on Saturday nights. He gave our mother, who lived with him and paid his modest bills, great joy. When she died, the family hired a live-in companion to ease his decline. For half a century he had been smoking unfiltered Camel cigarettes. His body, skin, voice, teeth and movements all showed the effects of his habit and each of his siblings worried about him because he was the family favorite. I especially felt guilty, as a doctor and as his brother, for not having tried harder to convince him to quit smoking.

"Do folks still take you for Hugh Hefner occasionally?" I asked, as Brody emerged from his berth the next morning in his quilted garment. Although he did look similar to Hugh, I was sure that his smoking jacket played a key role in this misidentification and that Brody loved masquerading as Hugh.

"Yeah, last week in Owosso some guy asked me that."

"What did you tell him?"

"Same thing I usually do. I said, 'Yes, my friend, and, how are you? Any action in town? That usually stops them. If it doesn't, I usually get the name of a good bar or two.

"Got some new Docksiders for this trip,'" Brody said as he

47

stood to show me his new shoes. "They make my feet feel good." He lit a Camel and extended it to me. "Wanna puff?" he asked. "Like we used to do on the way home from school. Eh? Remember?"

I took a puff and Brody laughed. It was the heartiest of laughs, raucous and real. I remember as a little boy wanting to be like Brody, but most of all wanting to laugh like he did. So, I copied him. Every time he laughed, I laughed. Now, years later I can say his laugh is my laugh.

"Do you remember the time we got everybody laughing in church?" Brody asked, as we stuffed his luggage in my sports car.

"Do I ever!" I said. "You mean, when *you* got everybody laughing?" I corrected. "Tell me what you remember."

"Okay. I remember sitting in church with you and Mom waiting for Cathy Irons' christening to begin." Brody had an amazing memory, the best in our family, by far. "It was about noon and I was really hungry, and we were talking about food and all of a sudden you said real loud and as if you were a real authority, 'lima beans give you diarrhea.'

"Well, that struck me as funny," Brody said. "I thought that was the funniest thing anybody had ever said, especially in church. It still is funny," he murmured.
"Then you repeated it. Remember? And suddenly both of us were laughing like crazy."

"Yep. It must have struck us both as hilarious because we were rolling on the floor, not really, Mom, and within a minute or less everyone was laughing else was too."

"Did we get in trouble for that?" I asked. "I can't remember."

"Mom was embarrassed, but she couldn't really punish us because laughing is a good thing, and everybody was laughing. But she told Dad and after dinner he said, "Go to the cellar, boys."

"Did we get spanked for that? Gee. I'd completely forgotten."

"Sorry I told you the end of the story then, Little Bro."

When we climbed into our berths that night, Brody yelled to me, "Don't start laughing now or tomorrow I'll buy you the biggest bag of lima beans I can find and make you eat them all." I went to sleep smiling and less concerned about how we were going to fare confined together in a rather small space. Brody made me feel at ease.

In the morning, I turned on the radio so Brody could hear about the midge flies from an authentic weatherman, rather than from his little brother. When the weather report ended, Brody looked worried and said, "What's that mean for us?" I explained to him what I had gone through the day before, gesturing at my swollen face as proof, and said we would have to stay put for safety sake until the Coast Guard gave us permission to leave. "We'll have to find ways to amuse ourselves," I said with false enthusiasm.

"I remember how I amused myself one morning at home," Brody said. He loved to talk about the old days. "We were little guys, probably eleven or twelve then."

"Oh yeah," I said, "and what did you do?"

"You should know. You were there. Mom and I were eating oatmeal for breakfast when Dad came into the kitchen to get his coffee." Brody spoke his last word 'coffee' in a whisper and suddenly the atmosphere had changed; our storyteller was clearly frightened. He didn't always think his stories through to their conclusions. In this case, we were to learn, he had talked himself to the brink of a traumatic incident, the consequences of which he had carried with him for close to sixty years. He paused, gathered his thoughts and his courage, and continued.

"I put some oatmeal on my spoon and flicked it at Dad. I guess it kind of divided into two globs while it was in the air flying at him because two globs hit him, one on each lens of his glasses. It was a one-in-a-million shot and it looked hilarious. Even Mom couldn't help but laugh at her husband, although she was trying not to. But it was scary too because we didn't know what Dad was going to do. We just knew how pissed he was. His face turned red and he stormed out of the kitchen. I had never seen him move so fast."

"And that night we got the razor strap, right?" I asked. Brody shook his head. "You did, but not me," he said quickly and quietly, as if he did not want anyone to hear. I put my hand on Brody's knee and waited. Finally, he said in the smallest voice of all, "after he sent you upstairs, he hit me with his shillelagh ... on my head ... only on my head over and over."

As I said, Brody never hugged, but I could not help but put my arms around him and hold him when he stopped speaking. For a few brief moments he might have felt as if he were a nine-year-old boy again, bleeding from the head, but protected finally in his brother's arms. He offered no resistance to my embrace. He even reached up with both hands and patted my shoulders. It was as if he were comforting me, not the reverse.

"Did you ever tell anyone about that beating," I asked, slowly letting go.

"Nope. This is the first time I ever told anyone. I was afraid that nobody would believe me. They'd tell Dad and I'd get it again."

"You didn't even tell Mom?"

"Nope."

I had no doubt that Brody was telling the truth. He didn't seem to grasp the abstract nature of a lie so, to my knowledge, he never told one.

Brody had retreated to my cabin after finishing his horrifying tale and stayed there asleep until I was ready to turn in. As I entered my cabin, Brody said, "Mind if I stay with you tonight?"

"Yes, of course, you may," I replied. "Are you okay? Do you want to talk? Want me to make you a cup of tea? A scotch perhaps?"

"No, I'm fine. I'll be good tomorrow."

He was just spent from the enormous effort it took to relive that incident. He got up the next day and carried on as usual, demonstrating to me yet again how resilient and strong he was. It would take more to keep Brody down than the herculean effort he made to regurgitate the memories of that 58-year-old beating he had been lugging around by himself all that time.

"Okay," I said. "I know you're a tough guy, but if you need anything during the night, just call me. I'll be right here."

As soon as I turned the light out, Brody said, "There's one

thing about the Oatmeal Bowl that I didn't tell you yet."

"What's that?" I asked and held my breath.

"I've always thought that what I did that morning was the reason they sent me to that school for ten years. Do you think that's why?"

"No, I don't. It wasn't. Why would you think that?" I gasped.

"Because Dad was so, so mad at me and it was the quickest way for him to get rid of me."

"But, Brody, that's not why you went to Cleveland. It was not to get rid of you … Listen, Big Bro. It's two in the morning and we have a week to talk about this. Let's you and me get a good night's sleep. We'll have a dip in the lake in the morning, a Cuban cafécito, and then some pancakes. And while we're doing all that, I'll be telling you everything I know about your school and why you went there. Okay?"

"Yeah."

"Okay, Brod. Sleep tight."

Quiet descended, except for the lapping of the lake's gentle waves against our hull. Ten minutes later, I called Brody's name quietly. No answer. I wanted to be sure he was sleeping soundly before I slept. He was sleeping like a baby as he always did. His conscience was clear.

The next morning, I was the first man up. I pulled on my swim shorts and made the coffee. I was sitting in the cockpit, basking in the warm sunshine and listening to the breeze tickle the pine needles when I heard a thump, a muffled *'Goddamn it,'* and then watched Brody struggle to climb the ladder to the cockpit. I didn't offer assistance because he had waved me off the night before when I offered him a hand. He was wearing only his pajama pants. The skin on his chest, back, and arms looked like Egyptian parchment, yellowish and brittle. He looked ill and twenty years older than his actual age.

"Everything okay below?" I asked, referring to the thump.

Without answering the question or even acknowledging that he heard it, Brody shuffled to the stern, dropped his pj pants, and cannonballed into chilly Lake Michigan. His frail frame didn't produce much splash, but his shriek must have awakened the entire yacht club. I followed him in.

Fifteen minutes later we were lounging on deck in dry clothes and sipping our Cuban cafés. "I'm going to go make some pancakes," I said. "Why don't you come in with me?" For several minutes I had been trying to think of an opening line that would entice Brody back into the conversation we had last night. He had to be in the right mood to talk about serious matters. Finally, I thought I had a good line. "You know Mom loved you best, don't you?" I asked.

"Really? How do you know?"

"All four of us could see it. But we didn't mind. She had enough love to give lots of it to everyone. When you were eight or nine, Mom started to worry about you because your teachers said you were not catching on to your lessons fast enough. She suggested that you should be tested to find out why you were falling behind. So, Mom asked Dad to get you an appointment with the best kids' doctor he could find, and *that* is why you went to Cleveland and saw Dr. Sloan.

"After he ran some tests on you, he wrote Mom and Dad a letter saying that you were 'strong, healthy, attractive, and socially well-adjusted. That meant that you got along well with kids of your age. He also wrote that you were mildly retarded, but he thought it possible that you could live on your own someday. Finally, he recommended that we look into schools like St. Thomas because there your IQ would place you among the smarter students in your class. Whereas, in a regular public school, your IQ would place you low in your class and you would have to struggle constantly to keep up." I paused, took a deep breath, and said, "And that's the truth, the God's honest truth, and nothing but the truth."

"Really? Cross your heart and hope to die?"

"Cross my heart," I said, making the sign. I've got a copy of the letter Dr. Sloan wrote. I'll show it to you."

I went over this with Brody two more times using different vocabulary and speaking slowly. I knew better than anybody how to talk to Brody, but I couldn't be sure he had grasped the key fact: that neither his mother nor his father had ever tried to get rid of him. My instincts told me that despite my protestations, Brody still saw a cause and effect connection between his behavior at that breakfast table long ago and his evaluation by Dr. Sloan that resulted in his moving away from home for ten years to attend a special school.

It bothered me that Brody had lived much of his life under the misapprehension that his special education was really a punishment. I wanted him to know that his mother loved him and was unwaveringly loyal to him all her life, and that his father was at least financially generous to him. If there is a Heaven, I thought, Mom is there and deserves to know that her favorite son, Brody, finally appreciates all she did for him.

As we worked in the small galley making breakfast, I said, "I had the impression over the years that you liked St. T's quite a bit, that you were happy there. Were you?"

"Yeah, it was okay, kinda fun," Brody said.

"Well, you can't like punishment, can you? If you liked it, it wouldn't be punishment."

"Are the pancakes almost ready? I sure am hungry?"

After breakfast Brody thanked me and handed me his spotless plate. It was a lifelong habit. Everyone in our family had tried to get Brody to drop his custom of polishing his plate with his tongue and his napkin after eating, but to no avail.

What a morning it had been! Talking seriously with Brody required patience and concentration and the need to remember always that inside that sixty-eight-year-old body was an eleven- year-old boy with a short attention span. It seemed to me that Brody also tired more quickly than he used to. But that morning his clean dirty plate popped us back into our normal groove. "Do you want to take a walk?" Brody asked. "Check out some of the boats, get a sandwich?" So, we walked.

As soon as we were off the dock, Brody lit up a Camel. He never liked exercise and now I knew why he suggested the walk. "Seen any good movies lately?" I asked.

"Yeah. I saw Bruce Willis in *Pulp Fiction* the other night." And then he was off, explaining the plot in detail, the gore, and how cool Bruce was. "Did you ever see Armageddon?" he asked. "That was my favorite," and Brody treated me to a summary of that blockbuster. "Don't you think that if we had sent Stallone, Willis, Schwarzenegger, and Dwayne Johnson to Iraq right away, we'd be long gone from there?"

"Come on, Brody, they're movie stars. They'd be whining like a litter of kitties if they had to spend two weeks in the Iraqi desert with real soldiers shooting at them."

"Well, do you know anyone as strong as Dwayne? His muscles aren't fake. You can see them. And Arnold must be smart. He was the leader of California. And in real life, Bruce married the first female Seal, I think. These guys get things done," Brody said. For as long as he and I had talked about action heroes, I still couldn't tell if Brody really believed in them or just got swept up into the movies and wanted to believe in them.

"When you put it that way ... maybe we *should* send them over to Iraq," I said. Brody offered me a high five. We bought sandwich makings, had an afternoon nap and a swim before dinner.

Each morning our first order of business was to listen to the weather and the day's midge fly reports on the ship's VHF radio. The latter provided us our only excitement of the day. For the first three days we booed as the weatherman told us no activity was expected in our zone, but on day four Brody let out a hoorah when the radio suggested that our peninsula might see a major swarm in the afternoon. I promised myself that Brody and I would be aboard our craft with all hatches battened down that afternoon.

"Be careful what you wish for, Brody," I said. "It may come true."

"This is like a sci-fi film," Brody said, "except it's real. Has anybody been killed by a midge fly swarm? Boy, what a way to go!" Brody was clearly enjoying the anticipation of disaster and carnage while I battened things down and made the deck as secure as possible. When the midges arrived, we sat below deck in silence, listening to the slap-shot pings, thuds and bangs of thousands of insects being flung against the boat's hollow aluminum mast, its solid fiberglass hull and its teak deck. The worst of it lasted about 30 seconds; it was all over in ten minutes.

"Man, o man!" Brody exclaimed. "In all my life, I've never ever seen anything like that. It's been a little boring sitting around here, but that bug show made it worthwhile."

"That makes me feel good, Brody, but what makes a good "bug show" for you?"

"Oh, didn't you think it was cool? That strange piercing noise all the time in the same key. It sounded like Arab music and it was just right to make me scared. Come on, Blake, I've got some money. I'll buy you a sandwich for dinner."

It was almost impossible to keep the guy down. After three days of stark boredom and probably six packs of filter-free Camels, all it took to re-start his engines was a singing mass of midge flies.

"I'm glad Mom wasn't here though," he said.

"Why's that?"

"Because she was scared of insects of all kind. She used to pay me a penny apiece for all the flies I could kill. It really didn't make you mad that she liked me best?" he asked, referring to our conversation of yesterday

"Noooo."

"Really? I thought Sister Beatrice was her favorite because she was the only girl in our family."

"Oh, no, it didn't make us mad," I said. "Well, maybe sometimes. But we thought you deserved a little extra love and we were glad Mom gave it to you. She had enough to give to the rest of us too."

"Then how come she divorced Dad?" Brody asked abruptly.

"I've asked myself that question many times over the years, but yesterday I think you gave me the answer."

"I did?" Brody said, with a look of confusion and curiosity on his face.

"Do you remember what you said yesterday?"

"I said lots of things. How could I remember all of them?"

"The shillelagh incident did it, Big Bro. It unlocked the mystery of their divorce. I couldn't sleep last night because I kept imagining Dad hitting you on the head over and over again.

"Let me tell you what I figured out while lying there wide awake," I said. "Mom saw the bumps and cuts on your head and knew right away who was responsible. That was easy.

Your little brothers and infant sister were too small to beat you like that with a stick and Mom knew I wouldn't do that either because I idolized you."

"What's that mean?" Brody asked. I was pleased. His question meant he was listening.

"It means you were my hero too."

"I don't know when Mom picked up the first warnings that she might have married a strange man with a potential for violence. But, try to imagine how devastated she must have felt looking down at the condition of her little boy's head; try to imagine her agony as she struggled to admit to herself that her husband had repeatedly struck her beloved, ten-year-old, intellectually challenged son on the head with a stick as hard as iron. She must have been so angry and so repulsed that she couldn't stand to look at her husband, much less take his hand and go marching into their waning years with him. Divorce was not a consideration for Mom, it was an essential." As I spoke to him, Brody sat still at the navigator's table, looking sad and pensive.

"Back in those days," I explained to Brody, "divorce was frowned on and required an annulment, i.e. approval by the Church. Mom pushed ahead with the support of only her local priest. Meanwhile, Dad moved out and began making the rounds with hospital nurses and other sources of eligible females, while Mom remained at home with her four children.

"You might wonder, as I did, why she didn't take Dad to court because what he did to you, my big brother, was a punishable offense, i.e. Mom could have won the court case, no doubt about it. My guess is that she felt her first priority was protecting us kids from more abuse. She wanted to avoid the nasty publicity that can hurt kids when their parents air their marital grievances in public.

"So, that's how I think our parents ended up getting a divorce."

"I'm glad he died so he can't do that to anyone else," Brody said quietly. He sounded tired, but he apparently wanted to stay with the conversation. "Do you remember when Dad bought us boxing gloves for Christmas?" he asked. I nodded and he said, "That was real scary."

"How so?"

"I don't know. I remember him yelling at you, 'Get him! Hit him again.'"

"How old were we then, Brody?

"I was 14," Brody said. "I remember I was home from school for the third Christmas." I was impressed how Brody's allegedly underdeveloped mind recalled details of things that happened fifty years ago. "Mom was really angry when he gave us that present and her face got red whenever she spoke about it."

"And she almost cried she was so pissed when he made us have a boxing match in the living room."

"Remember," Brody replied. "She was very serious, and she looked back and forth at you and at me and said, "Remember this, boys: Your brother is your best friend in the whole world." She was kneeling on the floor down at our level. "You must always defend your brother and always take his side no matter what side he is on. And you must never fight against your brother because he is your own flesh and blood."

"God, Brody. That's amazing. Is that exactly what she said?"

"Yeah."

When I took the garbage out that night, I saw the four boxing gloves in one of those big, smelly cans that would be emptied into a garbage truck and hauled off to the dump early the next morning. She had taken a knife to the gloves and the stuffing was coming out of all of them."

Our mother and father had a fight of their own that night after the kids had gone to sleep. I could only hear bits and pieces of what they said because their room was down the hallway from mine. But I thought I heard Dad say Brody was a sissy and immediately thereafter I thought Mom shouted, "Get out of my bedroom!"

The following day, after being strafed by a relatively small swarm of midge flies and after once again cleaning the boat, Brody and I walked into town for an ice cream cone.

"I hope my speculations yesterday about Mom's reasons for divorcing Dad didn't upset you too much. I could find someone for you to talk to if you want."

57

"No, I'm okay. You know, she's been gone for over ten years and I still miss her ... but not with sadness, if you know what I mean."

"Yeah, I think I do, but I think it's easier to find one's way in life if you have a partner, someone you share everything with. I know you're a well-known figure in your town, and I know you have lots of female admirers in town and I'm glad you do have fun with them, but I've always wanted to know, Big Bro ... uh, could I ask you a personal question?"

"Blake," he said sharply, getting my attention. You sure are going around and around the bush. Ask me the question."

"Okay. Have you ever been in love?

"Yeah, once."

"Who was she? Did I know her, you Sly Fox?"

"Her name was Zanda Ozolin."

"Wow! Quite a handle! How come I never met her? Were you ashamed of me?

"No, but you never came to see me at St. T's." I hadn't gone to St. T's to visit Brody because I was too busy with sports and girls. I did not judge myself too harshly for essentially deserting him during our high school and college years because I was a typical, self-centered adolescent then. Honestly, I'm ashamed to say this but Brody was hardly ever on my mind during those years. Gaining one-hundred yards or more in a game was more important than spending a weekend with my handicapped brother. As we walked back to the boat licking our cones, I could not think of anything I had done for him or with him until we started taking our cruises together three years ago. I had not idled away my time, however. I spent ten years in med school, surgical internships, and residencies, during which time I totally neglected my mentally retarded big brother. I could never explain this to Brody, but maybe I could make amends.

"How long has it been since you last saw Zanda?" I asked.

"About fifty years," he said.

"Do you know how to spell Ozolin?"

"O-Z-O-L-I-N," he answered without hesitation.

"Do you mind telling me about her?"

"I met her my first day at St. T's. She had red hair and blue

58

eyes and freckles, and eight brothers and sisters and she was the youngest and the only "slow" one in the family. She was about as "slow" as me so that's why we got along so good probably. When we knew each other better, she invited me to Sunday dinners with her family. Two nuns would drive me out to the Ozolin's farm and wait for me to have dinner. Dinner was a little scary because the Ozolins were poor and argued a lot, real loud, but still it was nice to be there with Zanda. Except they all spoke a language called Lativan or Latvian, which only people from their real country spoke. Zanda was the closest friend I ever had. We grew up together at St. T's. We met when we were ten and said goodbye when we were twenty. They had an old, old tractor they taught me to drive and once in a while I drove Zanda into town to get an ice cream. So, for a little while we could go on dates like regular people. When I left St. T's I was so sad. I felt like a hollow person going back to Flint, like I was empty inside. I didn't tell her why I was sad, but she must have figured it was because I was leaving the school forever. And she was right, kinda."

"What do you mean 'she was right kinda?'"

"Zanda was pregnant," he said, whispering the last word.

"Holy Moses, Brody, you really are full of news this trip." Brody just shrugged. Did you ever try to see her again?" He shook his head. What a sad story! Well, don't keep me in suspense. What happened?"

"Zanda's oldest brother, Janis, was really steamed at Zanda and told her no way she could keep her baby. He said they couldn't afford the food and clothes and all the things you need to buy for babies. Janis and Zanda's mom tried to talk her into having an abortion because they thought it would be easier on her, but every time the word was used, Zanda said 'no, no, never, I'm not killing my baby'. They even called me and asked if I'd try to talk Zanda into it. I tried but, of course, I didn't know what to say and besides if she didn't want an abortion, neither did I. I felt sorry for her because during that call she told me how upset everyone was in their house and said they couldn't make her do what they wanted because she was the mother and she was already twenty-one. She was a stubborn little one. She had the baby and signed the papers the next day so somebody else has him now."

"No. He's almost fifty years old now, Brody. Probably he has some kids of his own."

"No, he's just a little kid who looks like me." Brody had difficulty appreciating the passage of time.

Changing the subject slightly I said, "But Mom and Dad never knew you were going through this hell?"

"Nope, they never knew because I only got two calls and the worst part is coming. After the baby was born, Janis called me again and said, 'Brody, listen to me you little peckerwood because I'm talking for the whole Ozolin family. You better not call Zanda *ever again*. And you best not write her any letters neither. You are never to contact her again in any way, you hear me? In Latvia, where we come from, Zanda's other brothers and me would probably kill you for doing what you did and then feed you to the hogs – and don't you forget it,' he screamed and hung-up."

"Oh man, Brody! There were six or seven men in that family, weren't there? That must have scared the bejesus out of you. So, what did you do?"

"I didn't tell anybody or do anything."

"You could have called *me*."

"But in those days, I didn't even know your phone number."

"Yeah, I know. I'm sorry, really sorry, I apologize for not being around very much for many years. I'm really sorry."

"That's okay. Brothers don't have to apologize."

"Would you like me to try to find her phone number so you can call her now?"

"Yeah," Brody said immediately, but then he hesitated and asked, "Do you think they would still kill me if I call her?"

"I don't think so. Almost fifty years have passed since they threatened to kill you. That's a long time. Who knows if any of them are still alive? If Janis was thirty years older than you then, he'd be almost one hundred now. I can't believe any of them, if there are any still living, would still be holding a grudge against you. I think we're safe enough, don't you?

"Yeah. Let's call."

Her unusual last name made her easy to find and before

long I was introducing myself to Ms. Marie Ozolin of Jefferson, Wisconsin. "Ma'am, my name is Blake Mahoney. I am the brother of Brody Mahoney, who was a frequent guest at your farm during the years he attended St. Thomas ..."

"Brody Mahoney. My goodness mercy! Who could ever forget Brody? No one in our family, that's for sure. Is he still alive?" Those two questions led me to imagine Marie heading for the shot gun hanging above her mantle. "Zanda is my little sister. She and me are the only two Ozolin still living."

"How is Zanda, by the way?"

"She's happy, as usual. Full of beans. You know, for many years Brody Mahoney was a swear word in the Ozolin family. Yes sir, it was! How is ol' Brody doin?" Although our conversation was a little disjointed, eventually I finished explaining to Marie why I had phoned and she replied, "Zanda lives nearby. I see her about every day because she doesn't have no phone. When I do see her, I'll find out if she would like to talk to your brother. How is Brody these days anyway? How's his health? Maybe she'll want to see him, maybe she won't. She's a handful that one. If you give me your phone number, Mr. Mahoney, I'll let you know her answer. Goodbye."

Back at the boat Brody listened passively to my report and said, "Time will tell, but it doesn't sound good."

My concerns about how my brother and I were going to coexist for a week on a small craft proved to be unwarranted. In fact, we had the best conversations we'd ever had. But things began to get quiet as time dragged on and we heard nothing from Maria about Zanda's verdict. What we did hear was the sound of each tick and each tock of the old ship's clock. Each metallic beat seemed to peal through the salon and echo off the bulkheads, reminding us that another second was about to pass into eternity. Luck and the little things in life conspired against us. We had a television aboard, but we needed a cable to get a picture and there was no cable available in the area. We slept so much during the day we couldn't sleep during the night, so we talked. Early one morning I asked Brody what time it was.

"I don't know," he said, "but the radio has been reminding

61

everyone to adjust their clocks back when they get up Sunday morning. Something's wrong with the time." About five minutes later, Brody, surmising I was worried, patted me on the shoulder and said, "Don't worry, Little Bro, they'll have their best guys on this problem because they're having the same trouble way up to Ann Arbor."

At three o'clock in the morning, Brody's comment seemed to sum up our situation perfectly: it made no sense. We had had midge attacks, no television, disrupted sleep, and now someone was tinkering with time. So, I looked at him and said, "SNAFU."

"What's that?"

"It's an expression they use in the Army. Situation Normal All Fucked Up. First letter of each word equals SNAFU." Brody loved the sound of it and suddenly The Laugh started. Mine followed and we laughed together just as we had all those years ago in the church.

After I turned the light off, Brody said, "It doesn't make sense that they would have sent me away to school for ten years because of one fling of oatmeal. I know that."

"Thanks for telling me, Brody. I'm glad you realize Mom and Dad were never trying to get rid of you. Mom loved you way too much for that. You know that, right?

"Yeah."

"And hopefully, knowing that will make you a happier person." I decided to shut up for a while. Several minutes passed. No noise or words emanated from Brody's forward berth. Ten more minutes slipped into the night.

"I love you too, Brody."

"Yeah."

The midge fly report the next morning said the restriction on operating pleasure boats was lifted as of 7 a.m. "I'm going up to the yacht club to pay our bill, Brody. Be back in fifteen or so. Then we can boogie on out of here – finally. Why don't you put on the jib?"

That was my cover story. Instead of paying our bill, I phoned Marie. She sounded less confused than when we last spoke. "Mr. Mahoney, Zanda has written Brody a note and put in it a sealed envelope. I will be happy to mail it to you if you wish."

"May I please come and pick it up? If you have a mailbox, I could just pick it up there so I wouldn't inconvenience you."

"That would be fine. I'll put it in there right now."

When I told Brody what I was going to do, he insisted in riding along. He said almost nothing on the way over. "Are you nervous?" I asked.

"Yeah."

I plucked the envelope out of the mailbox and handed it to Brody. He held it in both hands on his lap and stared at it for the next thirty minutes, all the way to the boat. I ran each gear out to the red line and was flying through the rural landscape, barns, farm equipment, front porches flashing by. I couldn't wait to get my boat out of that harbor. I slowed to the speed limit as we neared our destination and vowed not to ask Brody any questions. It was his business, not mine. Once on board, Brody went directly to his forward berth, leaving it to me to cast off the lines, hoist and trim the sails, cut the engine, and do the other chores associated with getting underway. But I was as content as I could be. Once out of the harbor, I climbed up to windward for better visibility, set our course for Mackinaw Island, one of Brody's favorite places in the world, and listened to the quiet that settles over a sailing craft after her motor is silenced. I felt her list and strain forward as her sails filled with the freshening breeze. I sailed for a couple hours, feeling subtle wind shifts on my cheek, making minor course corrections to keep the mainsail from luffing, scanning the scene beyond our bow for approaching vessels. I lunched on stale crackers and cold beer and thought about Brody lying on his berth alone with his thoughts. In mid-afternoon, I heard him go to the head and hoped that he would join me.

He did. He lumbered up the ladder into the cockpit and sat opposite me. "Grace is my favorite woman," he said.

"Mine too. Why is that?" I asked, making a mental note to tell my wife she had not lost her most favored woman status with Brody.

"Because with her it's easy to know what she wants and what she doesn't. She doesn't beat around the bush all the

63

time. Here," he said, handing me Zanda's letter.

"Brody, this is your private letter. You don't have to share it with me. "I'll understand completely if you don't."

"No, read it. I want you to."

On a pink card in a childish but neat hand Zanda had written:

Dear Brody,

I can't believe I am writing you after 48 yrs. I hope you are healthie and feel good and are happy. I remember talking about those things when we were young. Do you? My sister Marie said you wanted to come over and talk. I have to think about this because I have a friend who lost his wife two months ago. I do not want to hurt him – not now. So I am thinking I will say no to you. I just think that's better – for now. I'm sorry. I will say a prayer for you every day and hope you come back. Sinserly, Za

(your nickname for me) xxoo

"What a sweet, thoughtful letter," I said.

"The problem is that she says it's best to say no and then she says she hopes to see me. I don't get it."

"It seems that she is a little uncertain about her loyalties."

"What do you mean?"

"Pretend you are Zanda, just for a minute. You are 68 years old and suddenly your first boyfriend – your first love – walks into your life unannounced after an absence of half a century and asks you to meet him. That's bound to have a major emotional impact on you, isn't it? On top of that, you are concerned about your friend, the widower, which shows Zanda is a sensitive and loyal woman."

"Ah, you like her then. Really?" So, what do I do?

"You decide."

"Decide what? I don't get it."

"You decide whether you like your present life so much you would not want to change it by bringing a woman into it; or, whether you know in your heart that life would be better if Zanda were a permanent part of it."

"What do you think I should do?"

64

"I can't answer that for you. There's only one person in this whole world who can answer that."

"I'm glad she's alive and healthy. I'm happy that she remembers me and wants to see me sometime – maybe. Isn't that enough?"

"Yes, I think it is, Brod. Enough for now at least. Give it some time. Write her a letter once in a while and always send your regards to the widower."

"Why? I don't even know him."

"To show her you're a nice guy.

"Can I ask her to send me a picture?"

"After you've sent her a few letters. I'll be happy to come up with you, maybe at Christmas, and definitely we could invite her to sail with us next summer."

"Good, but now is now," Brody proclaimed, shooting his arms and hands into the air. "Now I hope we're heading straight for Mackinaw Island because I'm really looking forward to smelling some fresh horse manure and eating some of that famous Mackinaw Island fudge."

THE DANCER

A Recurring Memory

She floats up the gangplank like a strand of silk on light air; her dancer's carriage, elegant yet arrogant, casts a cautionary spell; her blue-black hair, sleek and severe, is drawn tight to a bun; her bare, olive-toned arms and feathery hands alight occasionally on the handrails for balance. An offshore breeze wafting up the ship's hull lifts her skirts as she places a toe on deck and long fingers on the first officer's extended forearm. Her dark eyes barely acknowledge his reflexive glance at her thighs or his welcome aboard. A man, observing this theater from a deck above, wonders, then shakes his head and lets it fall to his chest. No need watching the mule train of passengers who follow. She was what he had hoped to see.

~ ~ ~

When they were first married, Jeannie accompanied Jackson on his 'Croesus cruises', as she called them, because in their youth these voyages seemed so lavish. They ate and drank free, lounged in the sun, and grooved on the music into the wee hours. He sat perched atop a collapsible chair driving the band, laying down the beat, while she draped over a bar stool filtering out the real deals, who were few, from the barflies, who were many. She had learned that some men, off on vacation from their families, believed cruise ships to be full of opportunities, so she was ready for them. "Did your wife have to stay home to work?" Jeannie would ask when she spotted a pale halo on a ring finger. Jeannie loved to ambush the philanderers, to jab them with questions about their infidelities and Jackson knew why.

She had shared the dark secret with him the night they became engaged – after smoking a joint or two. She told him she had once seen her father with her mother's best friend, Mrs. Villatoro, half-naked on the tendril-patterned cushions of the squeaky back porch swing. "I was only ten, for God's sake," she said. "I was collecting leaves for a Girl Scout badge in the woods behind Auntie V's house." The writhing bodies had stunned her, she said, dropped her flat on her stomach. They had fascinated but repulsed her. She remembered being well camouflaged in her scout uniform but still feared being seen so she lay low and still until Auntie V moaned and giggled and they went inside holding hands.

"I've never breathed a word of this to anyone," she whispered to Jackson, "hoping my silence would erase the memory, but of course it hasn't." Instead, she found that the rhythmic squeak of a pump handle, the earthy smells of her garden, even things unidentifiable could fling her back across time where she could smell the dirt again and feel the pine needles pricking her chest as she tried not to look at her father's fleshy white ass.

"Our life was never the same," she said. Jackson held her hand as she recalled the silence that encroached on their household and her parents' disengagement from their intimate dances: their teasing, their private nicknames, the ease of their co-existence, all congealed in the chill that summer, then disappeared. "My damned Dad! He must have been discovered." Jeannie whispered.

"And what happened to Auntie V?" Jackson asked.

"Oh God! She died six years later on her cellar stairs. Rumor had it that she missed the second step from the bottom, fell backward, and snapped her neck on a riser – never moved a muscle after the fall. My Mom went to her service, but my Dad didn't."

To Jeannie's guilty relief, Auntie V's death released her. The wicked witch was dead; her spell, broken. "I couldn't shout hooray from the rooftops, but I did begin to feel better. Then, a little later, I discovered I could sing," she said, brightening at the memory. This was a natural love affair, her mother told her. The musical DNA of her maternal grandmother, who had studied at Juilliard, had survived, leapt a generation and spawned in Jeannie's pool. At seventeen she had a smoky contralto voice, a broken heart, and perfect pitch, nice credentials for a blues singer.

She learned about phrasing, breath control and interpretation, but mostly she just sang ... during long teenage showers, in the car, and with a jazz group on weekends. In college she got into minor keys, dissonance, and syncopation, sounds and off beats that reflected the lack of resolution at home. She found when she sang from the heart, allowing the loneliness she felt to prevail, she could hush and haunt a room, but she was unwilling to do that often. "It makes me feel vulnerable," she told Jackson.

"When I first heard you sing," he said, "I was touched almost to tears. It's one of my most memorable moments in music. I even remember what you said when I introduced myself to you after that set. You were still revved from the applause and you said, 'Yeah, I know you. You play so clean. I love your music, man.'"

~ ~ ~

"*Hombre, me encanta la musica.*" He heard the husky voice that night on the cruise ship as he returned to the bandstand. Even before he was able to associate it with the woman he had watched float across the gangplank that afternoon, he realized her first words to him had the same meaning as the first words Jeannie had spoken to him years ago.

Drummers pick up on rhythms like this. The lapping of waves, a woodpecker's vamp, the swaying of hips. If it's repetitive, there's a rhythm. Jackson returned to her table when they finished playing. "*Buenas noches,*" he said, pulling up an extra chair and placing it off her shoulder so she had to turn away from the two couples sharing her table. He wanted no interference. "Jackson," he said, extending his hand. "*Me llamo Jackson* – that's my name – and that's the end of my Spanish. "*No mas,*" he smiled.

"Well, *no te preocupes, Yackson.* Don't worry. I speak English and I do love *la musica.* You can really touch your toes to it."

"Yeah, it's toe touching music all right. May I ask where you are from?"

"I am from Madrid," she said, thickening the first 'd' and softening the second to a 'th'. "It is a city *muy, muy bonita* and *llena de vida*, full of life." She had lived life fully, perhaps too fully, Jackson thought, aware that this up-close impression was at odds with the apparition he had seen from afar that afternoon. But she sat, even half-turned in her chair, as she walked, buoyant, diaphanous, her posture in perfect plumb. In contrast to her lightness of limb, her face was somber, more Moorish than Latin. It was marked along the jawline by a trail of pocks, the vestige of an adolescence long past. The eyes were private, not-to-be-trifled-with eyes. They looked down a flat, broad-bridged nose that gave strength not beauty to her face.

Jackson took a chance. "Goya would have loved your face," he said.

"Goya?"

"Yeah, the Spanish painter," Jackson replied with the hint of a question in his voice. Did she not know him?" I'm not an expert, but I think he painted some Spanish royalty when he was young...before he got consumed with disaster and pestilence. I remember some portraits in the Prado Museum in Madrid, great faces."

"*Ah, si. Goya. Perdoneme,* but I didn't understand your pronunciation. You have visited *el Prado*?"

"Yes, I have. I was touring with Dr. John. Maybe you've heard of him. We played Madrid, Barcelona, and Sevilla. Didn't have much free time, but I did go to the Prado. Loved it," he said with emphasis.

"*El Prado es una maravilla,*" she said. "It is 'a marvelous', right?"

"We would say it is 'a marvel', but I agree, *es una maravilla, correcto*?"

She smiled at this linguistic somersault, a minor amusement. The smile rolled gently over her grave features forming fine crinkles at the corners of her eyes, soothing their intensity. It softened the set of her jaw and the vibe between them. Jackson returned the smile. It worked, he thought, like flowers on a weeknight. "Would you like to buy me a drink, Yackson?"

When she rose to leave almost an hour later, she extended her hand toward his lips in a courtly, antiquated custom.

Jackson, caught off guard, reacted by catching her hand in both of his, a response grooved in his brain since his days as a Little League shortstop. Then, looking into her eyes, pleading for some small signal that he was not making a fool of himself, he bent and bestowed a misdirected kiss on her watch. "*Buenas noches*," he said, unable to stifle a grin. "Ah, my dear Yackson," she said in her throaty voice, her hard-Spanish eyes softening again, "Good night"

~ ~ ~

"*Ah, my dear Yackson.*" He could still hear it. A come-hither farewell if he ever heard one. But what the hell are you doing, Jackson thought, slumped across the only chair in his steerage cabin. Leave her alone!

His mood, as often occurred after he had played well and hard, was losing altitude, letting down through the clouds of adrenaline and nervous energy. Playing drums could alter his mind. Maintaining a clean, relentless beat, hands and feet creating their own catchy embellishments, bearing down then easing back for contrast, tapping out accented triplets on the snare's sweet spot, then only on the rim or on a wood block, mouth involuntarily askew, then a Rich-type roll, left left, right right, slowly accelerating until the sticks are a blur, and the applause spontaneous: all this could leave him high. But afterward, off-stage and alone, he would sink to reality again. Jeannie called it 'rubbing the rosy off his glasses'. He thought of her and told himself again, "Let it go, man. This lady of Spain ain't worth it."

As the lusty glow of their youth cooled over the years, Jeannie had become the ballast in his inconstant life, a shelter from the craziness of the music world. She had given up her singing because singing the blues gave her the blues. She often left the stage not only sad, but even angry. "You know," she told Jackson once driving home from a late-night gig, "I don't blame Frankie one little bit for shooting Johnnie, the little shit. He deserved it." Jackson took note – a father's influence can last a lifetime. He did not argue the point.

The less she sang, the more she engaged in Jackson's career, booking his dates, negotiating his contracts, jumping on problems with the purpose of a pit bull. She was good at it, tough and knowledgeable and yet accommodating to other musicians' agents, as long as they kept their word. One lie, though, one false promise and she wrote them off.

"You know," he said to her one night as they were drifting off to sleep, "you make me feel protected."

"How's that?"

"You make me feel 'safe and sound' like my mom used to say."

"Hmm ... love you," she said wiggling backward into him.

~ ~ ~

The sense of security he felt nestled next to her never waned. "Hey, J, whaddaya say?" became the opening line of his almost daily calls to her when he was on the road. Whether he was sitting backstage in a theater in Nashville or killing time in a park in San Francisco on tour with Clapton or Toussaint or someone else, she was always with him. When he miscalculated a time difference and woke her, she never asked him to call back.

And she was always on his mind when he succumbed to temptation. Tipsy girls and women, enchanted by the music or by musicians, chatted him up, offered their favors, hustled him off to the most unlikely venues: a tanning salon once, a surprisingly spacious bunk in the cab of an 18-wheeler, a leather sofa in the office of a state legislator in Bismarck, North Dakota. But, plodding back to his rooms in the middle of the night, he always felt despicable and puzzled over why he repeatedly did this.

He would lie on the bed in his hotel and call home. The calls became a ritual, an unction to soothe his guilt. They would yak and laugh and he would tell her he loved her and before falling asleep he would recite the litany to himself: it really meant nothing; it was a harmless occupational hazard; he was not – never had been – even vaguely interested in an affair; and, Jeannie was not hurt by these one night stands because she never knew about them, thank God! These obedient sheep jumped out of their stalls when summoned and trotted docilely across his conscience – each bearing a piece of wooly truth – until he fell asleep.

It was true; the women meant nothing to him. He could

remember venues better than faces or personalities. But thoughts about the other truth, his carousing, taunted him. Risking everything for nothing made no sense. He wondered if it were an addiction like Booker and heroin, or some cryptic compulsion to prove something or to wreck his marriage. He had no answers. His only certainty was that eventually his infidelities would cripple their marriage. Even if he could keep Jeannie in the dark, he knew he could wreck it all by himself. Pushing up from his chair, he pulled off his clothes and slid into bed. I do this simply because I can, he concluded, as he lay his head on the pillow. If I can do it, I can stop doing it. I've just gotta kick this habit! *Ah yes, my dear Yackson, you really must.*

~ ~ ~

He was wading in flotsam, pants rolled up tight below the knees, strangling the calves. God, they ached. The feet were numb in icy water, but he waded on through construction debris: a saw, its teeth bared, a yellow crime scene tape, and twine, yards and yards of it, snarling his ankles, impeding his progress. Doggedly he pushed on toward a grand pavilion and the music. Gypsy cants, Sephardic, hoarse voices in minor keys, the percussion of stamping feet drawing him into deeper water. She drifted vaporously toward him across wooden boards, topless, back arched imperiously, fierce eyes locked on his. Her many hands and flexed wrists swayed above her head like October branches while her fingers made chestnuts click and snap, embellishing the perfect accented triplets rolling off her feet.

"I dreamed about you last night," Jackson said stretching out on a deck chair next to hers.

"I am flattered." She spoke without turning her face from the sun. The tell in her eyes was unreadable behind her extravagant sunglasses. "A woman does not appear in a man's dreams without reason, you know, and a man does not tell a woman he dreams of her without reason *tampoco*." The conversation had accelerated from zero to sixty in a bat of her hidden lashes. "I trust it was a pleasant dream."

"I dreamed you were dancing the flamenco in a grand pavilion on the water somewhere," he said, "and that your footwork was much better than my drumming."

She turned from the sun, abandoning her tanning devotion, and slowly removed her sunglasses to look at him. The eyes were hard again, suspicious.

"Is this a joke?"

"No. Why do you ask?"

"I *did* dance flamenco in Sevilla on the Mediterranean."

"Is Sevilla on the Med"? he asked.

"Wherever! But how do you know this if you even don't know my name?" She had coyly declined to give Jackson her name the previous night, even after he bought her a third drink and teased her about being mysterious.

"If we are going to discuss your presence in my dreams, such an intimate topic, I must first know your name," he said.

"For now, you may call me Marquesa". She returned to the cover of her sunglasses and looked away from him back into the sun.

"Marquesa. How wonderful! I am conversing with royalty. I knew it," he said to flatter her. Then, so as not to surrender too much leverage, "Or was that your stage name?"

"Ah, Yackson, you are the drummer from heaven, but you have a mean stripe. No, my name is Charlotta Ruiz Rosa, La Marquesa de Girona y Bourbon," she said in concession. "That is my full name and *titulo*, which you will not remember I'm sure. *Ahora*, tell me how you know I was a dancer of flamenco."

Jackson studied her. He saw tawny skin, probably protected from Spain's harsh sun and pampered; sinewy arms, veins tracing subtly around her biceps and down her forearms; muscular legs even in repose; luxuriant, raven-black hair, probably its natural color and a source of pride. It flew in the sea air, freed from its usual sleek discipline. Only the hands, willowy but worn, hinted at her age; mauve squiggles meandered across the long bones running out from wrists to knuckles. She had wrapped herself in a sheer pareu, orange and teal with black and white, open-mouthed fish, nibbling here and there and seeming to swim across the folds of the material as it rippled with the breeze. A small Macy's tag flapped occasionally from a corner at her knee. She had tucked the garment into itself a discreet two inches above the nipple line. Not high fashion, Jackson thought, not expensive. She wore no jewelry, not even a ring, perhaps because she seemed to be sunbathing conscientiously. Every inch of skin glistened with an oil smelling of bananas; she had positioned her deck chair perpendicular to the sun and angled her limbs and face for maximum exposure. She turned her head and flipped her arms at regular intervals for even basting. Jackson thought: she is around fifty, hard-working, disciplined, and physically active because she is quite fit for her age; she is organized, and calculating, but not wealthy or well educated. Had Jeannie been there, she would have given Jackson good marks for his insights, but he knew her observations would have been more refined and insightful than his. Her keen intuition gave her an edge over Jackson in this little game they often played.

"I *didn't* know you were a dancer," Jackson said. "How could I have known?"

"That is your secret apparently."

"My dear Marquesa, my dream makes perfect sense. You look like a dancer. You move like a dancer. You are Spanish, as is flamenco. I had just spent one hour flirting with you. Then I go to sleep and dream of you dancing. *Por favor*, is that not logical? Now tell me, how did you become the beautiful dancer you are?"

"I will tell you on one condition."

"Anything. I will do anything you ask."

"Invite me to lunch, my dear Yackson."

~ ~ ~

Lunch became a ritual, a rite of passage Jackson hoped. It was always late and long, Spanish style. Jackson ate absentmindedly and he fell under her spell. She ate with finesse, European style, her graceful left hand holding the fork inverted and ever so lightly, while her right hand, using her heavy dinner knife with the dexterity of a surgeon, sliced and diced and arranged delicate bites on the fork. Jackson admired her flair just as he admired hands sweeping a keyboard or dancing between frets, but it was the quantity of food she consumed that fascinated him, astonished him really. At every lunch she prepared lady-like portions of every offering on the buffet table: soup, cold or hot; green salad, fruit salad, pasta salad; meat, fish, and chicken entrées; breads and crackers with butter and dips; each luscious dessert and coffee, black. And, she showed no signs of appreciation, satiation, or self-consciousness. The food was there. It was included in the fare, so she ate. Peculiar, Jackson thought. It's like she doesn't get enough at home.

"I was a prodigy," she began. "In my region of Andalusia to study flamenco was an option in my private *colegio* – I think that is like your high school. It is part of our *cultura,* so I was drawn to it. Plus, I wanted to avoid swimming or bow shooting. No interest, *nada.* I was a natural, my teacher said, and I adored it." She paused to convey an artful arrangement of salmon, capers, and dill to her lips.

"So, you continued after high school?"

"I continued *in* high school. I was sent to a school of dance in Sevilla. I had the best teachers and trainers and, of course, I worked at it every day," she said with no accent at all.

"Do you still dance?"

"Ah, my dear Yackson ..." she hesitated and looked into the distance, promoting a wistful silence. "I dance in my room every day."

Dancers are actors, Jackson remembered reading. This was certainly true of the Marquesa. She was drama itself. She could summon a coquettish character with a bat of her lashes or a sensual turn of her shoulder, and then dismiss her with the cool tone of a single word, but Jackson found her transformations unsettling. He preferred Jeannie's straight talk. She always calls them the way she sees them, he thought as his attention returned to the Marquesa. "Do you mean that literally, that you dance in your room?" he asked.

"I mean I no longer dance for *el publico.* I dance for myself. I had a great following, especially in the south of Spain, but that story is for another time, my dear," she said tipping the last drops from her *café solo.*

"As you wish, but remember, you have promised to continue. We play from 9 to 1 tonight. Perhaps over a drink afterwards?"

"*Vamos a ver*," she said, "we shall see."

She did appear that evening at about 10 o'clock, early by Spanish standards, dressed simply in black and without much jewelry. She sat at an empty table. Jackson acknowledged her from the bandstand with a big American smile. She responded curiously by laying an index finger on her temple. Maybe it's a Spanish gesture, Jackson thought, meaning 'I see you; I caught your greeting.' Later, two gentlemen joined her, seating themselves close to her, one on each side. Surrounded. Jeannie could have handled them, he thought. Three drinks arrived and from Jackson's distant perspective conversation flowed. Another round, open-mouthed laughter, but no dancing. His attention flickered between the table pantomime he was trying to interpret and the pulse he was feeling through the drums; table to traps, traps to table as if there were a pulsating strobe in the room. He looked up once to find the Marquesa and one of the gentlemen had gone. They did not return during the break but reappeared as the band began its last set.

Jeannie did not go away though; she lingered in his thoughts. He wondered how often *he* was in *her* thoughts and if she had liaisons too. She was a free spirit, after all, and he was on the road often. As he beat out a lively tempo on the drums, his imagination swept him down a dangerous slope. The loneliness of her life in New York certainly could make her vulnerable to some smooth operator and living in a metropolis, shit … her afternoon trysts in fancy hotels would be practically undetectable. God, her life was made to order for infidelity, just as his was! Clapping suddenly shattered his fantasy. The set was finished. He heard the increase in applause when the piano player called his name and he responded with a riff that plunged them back into the chorus of their last song. The audience loved it, but Jackson said 'fuck me' under his breathe.

Ten minutes later Jackson approached her table. She was alone again. As she gestured for him to sit beside her, he took her hand and dusted a kiss upon it. "See, I'm learning, getting better."

"To be authentic, my dear Yackson, you never touch your lips to the hand," she instructed. Also, not to the cheeks." Jackson smiled; her accent made 'lips' sound like 'leaps'; it almost rhymed with cheeks. "Sadly, you kiss only the air ... or the lips," she added as an afterthought. "Lips are for lips" (leaps are for leaps), she instructed. Zero to sixty again, he thought.

Perhaps the red wine she drank that night inverted her sense of modesty or put her inhibitions at bay. Whatever it did, as promised, she rolled out the dream-like tale of her career. It was full of gypsies, handsome guitar players, rapid passages of music and lovers, scarlet and black scandal, castanets and minarets and, above all, *el baile,* as she always referred to the flamenco. It was set in the clubs and theaters of Cadiz, Sevilla and Malaga with an occasional performance before royalty in Madrid. Jackson ordered her another Rioja at last call. They remained alone as the bar closed around them, but the Marquesa was undeterred. She had been a star, she said, at least among those in Spain who were aficionados of *el baile.* She had twice danced for the King, had a fling with a bullfighter, a fight with the tax authorities, and a marriage to the Marquis de Girona. Jackson, a son of White River Junction, Vermont, sat sipping a beer, listening and imagining: the smoky bars and plush theaters of Andalusia, Spain itself, hot and exotic, and this sultry, suspicious woman, who had loved and labored and been a part of it all. It made him feel as if he had spent his life in a monastery. Then, as quickly as she had begun her story, she stopped. "Walk me home, my dear Yackson. I have had too much Rioja. I have a headache and must sleep. *Por favor,*" she said warmly, smiling briefly and sliding her hand into the crook of his arm. When they reached the lobby, she kissed him on the neck below the ear and lightly descended the stairway to her cabin.

~ ~ ~

Their brief song was a rhapsody, irregular and improvised during the last days of the cruise – deck chair rendezvous, lunches winding through the past but skirting the moment, solitary siestas, and Courvoisier after midnight. They were in sync and yet a covetous tension hummed between them. He

could not find the key to free her – for more than a delightful moment now and then – from the protected preserve she seemed to prefer. He was inhibited by her presence and her exotic past. Her title and poses jostled his instincts, made him feel gullible and green. One minute she would raise the veil, soften her eyes, place a hand on his, and listen as he told her risqué tales of the music world, onstage and off. *No me digas* – you don't say – she would exclaim kittenishly. The next minute she would look away and the veil would rise again, eyes wary, her hand withdrawn and cool on the sweaty surface of a glass. In neither persona did she ask Jackson about his life outside music. Jeannie would have. She used to find out all there was to know about her onboard hustlers. But the Marquesa was indifferent to his biography. Perhaps, by refraining from asking about his personal life, she meant to keep the door to hers well shut. Jackson could dig that. Their no-pry agreement was keeping her a safe distance from his world too, but it was also keeping him from her cabin.

Time was running out, however. Jackson knew the Marquesa held all the cards and had put him into an alien role. He had always played the part of the hunted, which he felt he had mastered; he was never the hunter, which he was learning required much more skill. As he wandered back to his cabin it occurred to him that the closer he came to being rejected, the more he wanted the Marquesa. Denial and desire linked so irreconcilably. What a shame, he thought, as he stepped into his cabin alone.

~ ~ ~

"So, what's life like in Espana these days, for royalty that is?" he asked one morning as they lay sunning on a lee deck.

"Are you really interested in that? We are not full of surprises. We have our affairs and scandals like every people. We just do them on a grander scale, and we are discovered by paparazzi. Nothing stays a secret for long," she said from behind her large sunglasses.

"Well, tell me a secret, Mata Hari. What is the King really like? Do you know him?"

"I have met him, the first time with my husband and mother. The second time, thirteen months later, he

79

approached me, called me by name, and asked after my mother. I was impressed. Of course, some magazines say he is a *mariposa*, that he has his favorites among the handsome palace guards.

"What's a *mariposa*?"

"For *mariposa* I think you say butterfly, no? The gay man who flies from flower to flower, polluting each one."

"I think you mean 'pollinating', Marquesa, but I understand. So, the King of Spain is gay?"

"No, no, my dear Yackson. I tell you on good authority it is not true, but the Prince is. He has the Queen's looks, her mannerisms, her interests in the arts and fashion. He is a lovely boy." As she spoke Jackson admired her contours and imperial profile, canted precisely toward the sun. Her chest with its sheen of fruity oil rose and fell, twice for every roll of the ship. "I would love you to rub some lotion on my shoulders and back," she said as she rolled over.

"Do you know New York City?" he asked as he began to rub.

"Why would you ask that?" she said casually, but he felt the muscles tense in her neck.

"Just wondering." He allowed a long pause to widen between them; he wanted her to answer. "I work there often," he said finally, preferring not to disclose that he actually lived there, and paused again for her response. "Just curious."

The Marquesa waited several beats. "Curiosity can kill the *gatito*."

"Curiosity is also responsible for advances in science, the arts, and many other human endeavors," he said as he slipped the straps of her bathing suit from her lean shoulders to apply more lotion.

She rolled over again, swung her toned legs to the side and faced Jackson nose to nose. He could feel her breath; a stray hair tickled his forehead. "*Hombre*," she said, "you are not now thinking of advancing science."

"I always favor progress, Marquesa. The slower we move, the more we lose." He said these words semi-seriously while staring at his reflection in her dark glasses. While her eyes were hidden, her lips betrayed an expression of amusement, he thought, or perhaps acquiescence, but his question remained unanswered.

~ ~ ~

The entertainment director radiated an astringent lime fragrance. He stood too close when he conversed, and his busy hands were constantly plucking a hair from someone's collar or stroking his goatee. He had been touting the Grande Finale of the cruise for a week. Surf and turf served late, champagne on the house, formal dress optional, and gaiety – lots of gaiety. The band would play an hour later than usual, which curtailed Jackson's ultimate opportunity with the Marquesa and irked him generally. With each cruise he grew to hate these tinselly nights more. The counterfeit hilarity, the requests for schmaltz like *MacArthur Park* and *Muscrat Love,* the passengers' slurred compliments. The Finales used to drive Jeannie nuts, so she took to her cabin early.

The Marquesa did her one better; she never even appeared for it. He kept looking up throughout the long evening hoping to see her quirky, index-finger-to-temple greeting or to watch her effortless glide through the room. Damn, he thought, she's stiffing me on our last night. He banged away at the music, sticks becoming heavier, finesse vaporizing in the heat of his labor. Finally, they arrived at *The Party's Over*. He gave out a long sigh with his final flourish.

Minutes later he waved off his usual, a draught beer the bartender started to draw for him and asked for a scotch instead. "Tough night, Jackson?"

"Yeah. Too much Lester Lannon shit, man. I gotta get back to the City." A moment later watching the man's deft hands punctuate a bright blue drink with a paper umbrella Jackson asked, "You seen the Marquesa tonight?"

"She was here couple hours ago, but I was too busy to chat."

"One more, Phil. Make it a double," Jackson said, lifting his empty glass. He shoved back from the bar, grabbed his new drink, and stepped out on deck to feel the soft caress of Caribbean air one last time. He unbuttoned his sweaty collar, took off his shoes, and watched the moon slip behind an amethyst cloud. In time the moonlight and drink lifted the persistent tension of hope and allowed Jackson to consider his failed quest. He did not want to make excuses, but the Marquesa's whims and moodiness had thrown him off. She had escaped because he had never known precisely who he was courting. But now he could return to Jeannie a chaste man. This was a good thing, a legitimate clean start. 'This Could Be the Start of Something New' popped into his head. He hummed a few bars and stepped lightly down the passageway feeling like Gene Kelly.

~ ~ ~

"There you are, my dear Yackson." The husky voice flew at him from behind like a brick. He froze for an instant, a snapshot of a walker in full stride.

"Jesus, where have you been, Marquesa? What are you doing down here?"

"*Querido* – my dear – you are upset. Please don't be. I passed my last evening on the deck," she said. "So lovely, the sounds of the sea, the moonlight. I just preferred that to the *ruido* where you were. Sorry." As she spoke, her long fingers produced a key from beneath her shawl. "Isn't it fatal that we should meet by chance on our last night?" she asked. Moving gracefully in front of him she led him up several stairwells and down a passageway. Finally, she stopped in front of her door, inserted her key, and held her door open for him. "Do you believe in fate, my dear Yackson?"

His first step into her tiny cabin scattered his thoughts of chastity and redemption like butterflies. It was his answer to her question, his acceptance of her invitation. He stood shoes in hand, slightly tipsy from the scotch, as she rose on tiptoe, kissed him with moistened lips, then knelt before him and laid his shoes on the floor.

Shortly before dawn he rolled out of their narrow berth. "Be back at ten," he whispered, "so we can have coffee before we disembark. Okay? Do you hear me?"

"Hmmm."

At ten o'clock he returned to find her door ajar. "*Buenos dias,*" he called. No answer. He pushed in tentatively. No Marquesa. No baggage. Only his shoes on the pillow. In one he found a rolled piece of stationery. Slumped wearily on the

82

bed, he unscrolled it expecting an explanation or a word of farewell, but there below the ship's name was the Marquesa's theatrical adieu: a scarlet imprint of her lips. He held it for a full minute then let it fall to the floor.

As the months and years passed he discovered that she had left him more than a lipstick smudge. Memories remained, drifting like phantom companions along the edges of his mind. Why did they linger when memories of the others had escaped and vanished? It was not the love making that kept her there; their night had been nothing special. So, then it was the grace with which she moved that had cast such an enduring spell and her exotic story and the blush of theater she managed to daub on everything she touched. And yet, he reluctantly admitted, it was more than that; it was the sense of unease moving among those memories, a nagging impurity; it was a suspicion that he had been willingly duped that haunted him still.

~ ~ ~

A Recurring Memory

Several women descend from a Maids R Us van and, hunched against a gritty, winter wind sweeping down 1st Avenue, scurry toward a nearby bus stop. As they approach, a man stares vacantly out the window of a deli. He is preoccupied with thoughts of his recent separation, but irresistibly his attention is drawn to one of the women. She is bundled, wool cap pulled down, collar turned up, listing slightly under the weight of a Macy's bag, but still she moves effortlessly – like a dancer. Involuntarily the man rises from his chair, staring. The woman glides to a halt in line to board her bus. As she turns her back to the wind, the dark eyes, unprepared, glance through the deli window. The man races the length of the deli, then down the sidewalk but the procession of dirty windows and billboards is already filing slowly by him into traffic. Awash in fumes and breathless he spots her face again in the last window, an index finger lifting curiously to her temple.

AMERICAN DOVE

THE BEGINNING

Katherine Colombé, or Dove as she was known to all, lived a charmed and adventurous life. When Fate tempted her with opportunity, she would often jump at the chance to make something of it. This took courage, a quality she had in abundance, but it also took a special person, a gambler who was drawn to the excitement of risk. Dove had that quality as a young girl and never lost it. Even when she was in her sixties and concerned about her health, she preferred to return to her *belle France*, the land of her dreams and nightmares, rather than stay at home and miss out on something intriguing.

I met Dove at the Edith Berkner Elementary School in Savannah, Georgia, when we were six years old. One of my most prized possessions is a picture of us playing in the sandbox there. It was a present my mother gave me not long before she died, and it has travelled all over the world with me.

Dove and I went from second through eleventh grade together, always in touch but never best friends because our families were of different social and economic strata. For example, one year while I was caring for my two sisters, who eventually died of scarlet fever, and working as a substitute mother to my remaining five siblings, Dove was grooming her pony and attending private sailing lessons. Nevertheless, as we began our senior year, our friendship began to mature thanks mostly to Dove. She made me feel as if I were special and she had a knack for collecting people and converting them to friends.

I realized early that fall that Dove was no longer a schoolgirl. She was mature young woman who, under the influence of her father, was beginning to take an interest in world affairs. There were many bellicose parries and trusts in those days for her to study and learn from. Japanese torpedo boats attacked Russian vessels in Manchurian waters; the U.K. and France began talks on naval cooperation and signed an agreement recognizing joint control of the Hebrides; and, Germany passed legislation increasing the total tonnage of their fleet to keep pace with Britain's serge in ship building. In general, the great military powers were becoming distrustful of each other and many thought the entire world was moving toward war.

Despite these threatening developments, Dove enjoyed her last year of high school. She worked hard with her coach and became a better field hockey player and was elected co-captain of her team for her senior year. She also worked hard at her academics and received excellent grades. In fact, I think most of our classmates thought Dove would lead our class academically our senior year, but when all the figuring was done that honor went to me! She came to me right after the announcement was made and was so gracious.

"Congrats, Lottie," she said. "You deserved that more than anyone. God, you did an amazing job taking care of your brothers and sisters. I couldn't have done it, I know that. You are my hero, Lottie, really." Then she gave me a hug.

As graduation approached, Dove and I reviewed our options for employment opportunities. They were quite sparse. I encouraged Dove to shoot high because I believed she had what it would take to have some real success. I told her that it looked to me as if she had become the natural leader of our class. Her grey-blue eyes conveyed a sense of calm and competence. Her voice, pitched lower than most female voices, was soothing, even mesmerizing at times. Plus, she spoke with an enchanting Georgia accent. When I watched her put all those tools together to persuade someone to do something, I almost felt sorry for the victim.

Dove tended to think carefully about important decisions. I remember her saying to me often, "I've been thinking about that question you asked me last week ..." and then she would give me the benefits of her thoughts.

As time slipped by, she found herself thinking long and hard about her future. Smart, energetic women had to look hard for good career jobs and companies that would allow them to compete fairly for promotions. Among other qualifications, Dove was looking for a challenge and

86

something that would make her father, Arthur, proud.

The Colombé side of Dove's family had lived in Savannah for several generations, but her mother, Genevieve, was a French beauty with light blue eyes, perfect proportions, and a heavy French accent which sounded to my father, Tony Bianchi, like an illicit proposal. Genevieve gave birth to their daughter Dove in 1890 but she was much more interested in running her boutique than in raising her daughter. That responsibility fell upon Cary, a young black woman who had come to live with the Colombé family several months before Dove was born.

In the spring of 1898, Arthur and Genevieve were surprised, possibly even chagrined, to learn that a fifth member of the family would be arriving that fall. They named her Maribelle and called her Belle. During her early years, each Colombé family member tried to fit little Belle into his or her schedule, but they were only partially successful. In later years, Belle acknowledged that she didn't feel as if she knew her parents or her sister very well. Her mother continued to lavish time on her customers and her expensive women's clothing store. Her father kept watching his law practice grow and his private correspondence with American politicians and European intellectuals flourish. In fact, his ideas and treatise spread so quickly that even Arthur thought for a short time that he might be able to turn the tide in favor of neutrality.

Arthur was a particularly talented man. He was a maritime lawyer by profession, like his father before him. His colleagues and competitors agreed he had an enormous amount of legal knowledge stored in his big head, a superb command of English, and an incisive sense of humor, which his opponents learned not to provoke. There were many stories about his demeanor in the courtroom, but my favorite tells of the time a prosecutor cast an aspersion on the hair style of one of Arthur's female clients. Arthur interrupted him immediately. He turned to the judge for support and said, "I object to that unkind, personal affront to my client, and I hope that you would object also, Your Honor. Anyone who has allowed his hair to turn prematurely orange, as my opponent has, should not be allowed to criticize others." The Judge had to suppress his chuckle and collect himself before he was able to rule against the prosecutor.

The Colombés lived on Troup Square in a wonderful three-story house. Arthur had a kind word for everyone in the neighborhood, he was funny, and he was generous with those in need. After my sisters died, he used to come to our house on the first of the month and talk to my father in the park. I asked my father several times why he came over so often, but he wouldn't answer. The next time he appeared, I said, "Dad, are you in some kind of trouble?"

"No, Lottie, nothing like that. If you're still wondering about Mr. Colombé, he is helping me pay some of our bills, that's all. But, Lottie," he said sternly while pointing his finger at me, "you may not mention this to anyone, only me. *Capisce?*"

"Yes, I understand, Papa." I could tell it was a serious matter.

There were articles about Arthur in *The Savannah Tribune,* usually after he had been away assisting other lawyers try difficult cases. When Dove turned seventeen, Arthur had just agreed to go to New York to assist in a trial in which an eighteen-year-old young man was charged with stealing a $20,000 sailboat. The case was so unusual, and the defendant was so close to Dove's age that he asked if she would like to go with him. She jumped at the chance and enjoyed both the trial and the city so much that New York became her favorite city forever.

Early in her senior year, Dove began doing her homework in her father's study. She loved the room, its comfy dark blue leather armchair and sofa, its brick-red walls, and its deep-pile, intricately designed Turkish rugs. The pungent scents of her father's pipe tobaccos and cigars permeated the room and could transport her to faraway places.

She had taken to working there not because the décor appealed, but because it gave her good quality time with her father. They were so alike in important ways Dove told me several times. For example, Dove explained, "We both like learning. Dove especially loved the attention he gave her when he was fully engaged in teaching her. I was at a party at their house one Christmas and overheard a friend of Arthur say how proud he looked when he was with Dove. Arthur was not a man to discuss his feelings for his daughter, but he acknowledged the truth of the comment by saying, "And there are reasons for that, my friend."

Although the world was several years from the outbreak of war, storm clouds were gathering over Europe. A teacher at heart, Arthur piqued his daughter's interest in European politics by showing her where her great grandfather came from and why he left his country of origin for America. As a result of several years of study, Arthur had concluded that within a few years, most of Europe, America, and Canada would be fighting in a world war, which under the worst scenario would mean the sacrifice of thousands or hundreds of thousands of their native sons.

Gradually, Dove took to reading several papers like her father did and became very knowledgeable about world affairs. In the course of their discussions, her father taught her how to build her argument and how to deliver it with maximum impact. He was not upset when she disagreed with him, so long as she argued her opinion clearly and logically. In that room, father and daughter grew to know and admire each other and enjoy each other's company. When I think about him, he always has an enormous grin on his rather homely face, the one he wore when he first saw Dove after a long day's work.

One day after school Dove also showed me a big envelope filled with articles describing the appeal of Arthur's unique courtroom manner and how successful he had been while employing it.

"You should make them into a scrapbook for him," I suggested.

"No," Dove replied. "He never looks at that stuff. My mother just cuts the articles out of the papers and sticks them in there. Nobody ever looks at them. He *is* proud of his club, though."

"What's the club at all about then?" I asked, because Mr. Colombé was a kind of mystery man to me and I wanted to hear as much as I could about him.

"Well, about sixteen years ago," Dove explained, "he founded a club called The Gourds, made up of eleven men from here. They are different from each other in age, income, education, religion and everything. But they have one thing in common: they all enjoy learning. One of the guys is responsible for choosing a topic to be discussed at the next meeting. He learns about it, gives a little talk about it, and finally leads a discussion on it."

In Savannah, being a Gourd member had become a status symbol, and there was a long waiting list of folks who wanted to be members. However, until one of the founding members died, moved, or resigned, they decided to take no more members – with one exception.

From the time she was a little girl, Dove was her father's hostess at the Gourd meetings. Genevieve made appearances only occasionally because she was often busy at night promoting her boutique In any case, by having a perfect attendance record, Dove earned the role of chief hostess. She remembered as a little girl standing next to her father as the Gourds arrived, each throwing his hat and gloves on the piano bench, then turning to greet her. Some shook her hand, others brought her a little, inexpensive gift, but they all made her feel like a princess. Of course, in the beginning, she didn't understand much of the substance of their meetings, but as she grew more knowledgeable and confident, she engaged in their discussions more frequently, always offering the young, feminine perspective on the issue at hand.

On a cold October night, Dr. Ryan rose and said, "Gentlemen, I have spoken to each of you individually – except for you, Arthur – about the resolution we are about to vote on. Having heard no objections, I hereby ask that all those in favor of awarding Miss Katherine Colombé a lifetime membership in the Gourds, say 'yea.'" The chorus was loud and-clear. "Those opposed" ... silence.

Dove was so surprised and touched that she almost cried. She didn't though, because her father said women should not cry in public, especially when they're happy, because it makes them look weak. When the meeting was over and Dove had thanked them all, she and her father sat down together in his study, as they often did, to discuss the meeting.

"Was that a surprise to you, really, Papa?"

"Yes, it was, Honey." He was beaming. "Congratulations. I'm very proud of you."

The next morning, Dove asked him, "Papa, do you think Mr. Stuart is smart?"

"Yes, I do," Arthur answered. "I think he is one of the wisest Gourds. Why do you ask?"

"Oh, nothing," she said as she pulled on her jacket, kissed her father goodbye, and was out the door.

That morning I was walking by Dove's house just as she opened the front door and headed to school. This happened occasionally. We would easily fall in step and walk the two miles to school catching up on things, but that morning was different. Something clicked. We communicated and I think we felt we could trust each other because we had known each other so long.

I said to her, "Do you realize we are seventeen years old and have known each other for slightly more than 10 years? That's 62.5 percent of our lives."

"Did you just figure that out?"

"Yep. Divide 16 into 10. I'm pretty good with numbers."

"I guess so," she said. "Tell me, Lottie, have you ever met Mr. Stuart, the one who is a member of The Gourds?"

"Yes, my father does yard work and snow shoveling for him. Why do you ask?"

"Well, he said to me the other night, 'Don't be afraid to be original.'"

"He said that to you?"

"Yeah, but you know how he is … always serious and deep in thought."

"Yeah, but he's a smart guy. That's a pretty interesting piece of advice, actually. What's it mean?"

"I think it means 'be your own person.' But I can't just walk outside and, you know, be original. How do I do it?"

I thought about it for a moment, and then said, "How about if you go ask Coach Dillan if you can try out for the boys' basketball team this winter. Last time we talked you were angry because there was no girls' basketball team, so you

91

weren't going to be able to play."

When Dove didn't say anything in reply, I asked, "Is that too original for you?"

"No. It's a great idea. Thanks, Lottie. I'll go see him today or as soon as possible and I'll let you know what happens."

Dove prepared for her interview with Coach Dillan the way her father would have prepared for a trial. The next day Dove knocked on Coach's door first thing in the morning feeling a bit groggy but prepared and reasonably confident. When he shouted, 'come in,' she walked in, looked him in the eye, and said, "Hi Coach, have I got a great idea for you!"

"What's that?" he asked.

"I'd be very grateful if you'd let me try out for the men's basketball team next month."

Coach put his feet up on his desk, laced his fingers together behind his neck, and thought for a moment before replying, "Nothing against it in the rule book. They must have forgotten to mention it." He thought some more and then asked, "Are you any good?"

"That's for you to judge, Coach, but I bet I can get you ten points a game, minimum."

"Well, I guess it won't hurt none to give you a trial."

Needless to say, Dove played basketball for the boys' team that year, and when late winter rolled around, Coach Dillan asked if she'd like to play for the boys' field hockey team that spring. After a long talk, she thanked him but decided to play on the women's field hockey team for her one remaining season.

Within two weeks of Dove's talk with Coach Dillan, both of my sisters were dead. I had taken care of them to the end so, of course, I thought I must have killed them. I relived every single thing I did for them wondering what I had done or failed to do that resulted in their deaths. Having them gone and out of the house was such a relief, and yet thinking that thought added to the guilt. Finally, it all came down to a little saying that danced in my head all day long: POOF *and they're gone*. It captured my feelings, the simplicity and the finality, of that complicated and indelible act. The following week, I stopped at Dove's house on the way to school and we walked the rest of the way together, a custom we continued right up until graduation. Our friendship developed during those morning walks to school as we began to share our thoughts and concerns and to trust each other. Finally, years later, when I arrived at Auberny on the Western Front, and witnessed death by the hundreds, my little POOF-saying came back to me and eased the pain again.

I feel certain my life would have been different had I not stopped at Dove's house that morning. I have become a fatalist over the years. We don't control the real big things that happen to us. We marry the man who helps us to our feet after a fall on the ice; or a family loses two out of eight siblings to illness. Why them and not me? So much in life seems to be random.

It was June 1910. Graduation was approaching, and Dove was still waiting to hear if she had been accepted into a nursing program in New York City. The program was devised by doctors and nurses employed at the Presbyterian Hospital in New York, which was considered by many to provide the best nurses' training in the world. Dove tried to discuss her interest in a nursing career with her father but, uncharacteristically, he would not be drawn into it. She felt certain he was opposed to it, but she did not know how adamantly or for what reasons. She had no secret agenda. In fact, she had backed into the idea of nursing almost by default as it was one of the few professions in which women were accepted without discrimination and could aspire to reach positions of responsibility.

My future was even hazier than Dove's because I not only had no job, I didn't have any idea what I wanted to do. Dove and I thought about going to nursing school together, but the sight of blood made me nauseated and being one of eight kids taught me that I didn't want to be a teacher either. Since teaching and nursing were the only two professions for women in those days, I felt stymied.

I was sitting at the kitchen one afternoon feeling sorry for myself when my father came in, looked at me, and asked in his heavy Italian accent, "Whatsa mat?"

"Nothing," I said.

Ignoring my mood, he replied, "I think I have a good lead for you. You should look into the newspaper business. You're smart and always able to get people to talk to you. That's what being a reporter's about, I think." He said one of his customers had a brother who worked for the *Atlanta Journal,* a really good paper. In short, that's how I got the job. I was not to be working as a reporter, to be sure, but rather as a gopher in the Art Department. I was so green I couldn't understand my own job title, and my salary was so low it would hardly keep me in Coca-Cola. But I was free of my five siblings and living in a real city. Lastly, I discovered a distant cousin working in the same office. Our job was to provide photos for the stories the reporters wrote. My cousin loaned me money, showed me the ropes, and let me use his extra camera. He also introduced me to his friends and helped me get through a long bout of homesickness. He was a lifesaver.

Arthur worried about his wife's relatives who lived in the countryside outside of Paris. He even asked if I had grandparents living in Italy, which I did not. He complained to Dove that he couldn't get her mother to focus on her own parents' safety. While in his presence. Genevieve would listen, he said, and offer to write her family about moving to the U.S., but as soon as she was on her own, her thoughts turned toward problems closer to home and more immediate. Arthur told Genevieve he was anxious about Dove too.

"I could easily imagine her inquisitiveness and passion drawing her toward a war just to experience it," he told Genevieve. "And if she had a nursing degree, it would be all the easier, I presume. That's why I haven't encouraged her to pursue the nursing." He paused momentarily and studied the confusion and concern on his wife's pretty face.

"I don't mean to scare you, Honey, but I'm coming to the conclusion that this war is all but inevitable. I've been discussing it and its effects on the U.S. with some of my pen pals, and you should know that not all of them agree with me. Now, about Dove," he said, returning to his most important subject. "I don't think we should tell her how concerned I am. She and we are a long way from having to make any decisions about war, so let's just watch for a while. Okay?"

"Oh, Arthur, I think you're right. War is coming. That's why this is so frightening, but I agree, for the moment, let's wait and see. We don't even know if Dove will be going to school."

"Any school that didn't take her would be stupid."

Three days before graduation Dove received an acceptance letter from the nursing school, leaving her to face the most difficult part of the application process: telling her father what she intended to do. While walking to school the next morning, Dove and I tried to devise the most persuasive way to convince Arthur that this was the best option for her. After school, Dove wrote down points she wished to make and how she would express them. Then she memorized her words so that in the middle of her spiel, instead of thinking about what she would be saying next, she could be watching for signs of how her parents were reacting to her words. This was a technique Arthur had employed successfully in court many times and had taught his daughter to use when engaged in important debates. No doubt he would be amused by the irony.

She decided to hit them with the news as they were walking home from church that weekend, in hopes they would be in a kind and forgiving mood.

"Mother and Father ..." she said.

"Uh-oh," her father interrupted, detecting a certain tone in her voice. He turned to Genevieve. "Honey, I think this is important."

"I have decided to become a nurse," she announced. "And I need your support. In fact, I need it more than ever because this is not going to be easy. I know you are not elated with this idea, Father, but I've thought it through carefully and it's what I want to do with my life now." She stopped talking momentarily, hoping for a positive response from at least one of them, but they were speechless. So, she squared her shoulders, took a breath, and continued. "I have my letter of acceptance from a fine nursing school, but they need to know within ten days if I intend to accept a place in their class. So, that means ..."

"Daughter," Arthur said in a comforting voice, "We

support you. We can tell you that right here, right now. We support you." He put his arms around her.

"Oh good, Father. You don't know how good that makes me feel. Thanks for trusting me." Then, as an aside, she said, "Someday you'll have to tell me why you are so opposed this idea."

"Thank you too, Mother. Now that I know you two are behind me, I'm going to try to enjoy the fact that we have made a decision and I have a career in front of me.

"It's that and much more, honey, and I know you'll be great at it," her mother said. The two women in Arthur's life seemed to be moving closer together as Dove's departure time approached. Genevieve even stuck her head in Dove's bedroom one night and said, "I love you." Dove was skeptical of her mother's overtures, and with good reason. In the first letter I received from Dove in New York she said only that Arthur had taken her to the train station the day she left home. Genevieve had been at work and couldn't get away to say farewell. She ended the paragraph with these thoughts: "We just don't have much in common. I still hate rhinestones and I have no doubt that she still thinks girls' field hockey is vulgar."

To be fair, Genevieve did make one major contribution to Dove's life. From the minute she was born, she spoke to her only in French. Consequently, when Dove graduated from high school, she understood French as well as a native and could express herself on most matters with ease.

Life went on. Arthur and Genevieve attended to their businesses while keeping a weather eye out for signs that the storm was gathering. Had he voiced his fears that his daughter would be killed in a war, one might have reminded Arthur that there was no war, at least not yet. To Arthur, that was true but short-sighted. He thought the odds good that we would be at war within the decade and that the smallest political spark could set it off.

WAR

The first day of Dove's nursing career was memorable. All eighty members of the new class were following a school administrator from their dormitory, down into the subway for a three-stop ride. At the third stop they were to exit the metro and cross the street to the hospital where they would be working. In the middle of the pack, Dove was trying to maintain her position by staying close behind the classmate in front of her as they climbed the subway stairs. Her classmate was moving fast, head up, scanning the waves of pedestrians flowing down the concrete steps at her. Perhaps the girl lost her concentration or tripped. No matter, really, how it happened. What mattered was that she didn't lift her foot high enough to make the step. Instead, she drove her toe into the concrete riser and shot forward like a cannonball. With two armloads of books, she hadn't a prayer of breaking her fall and caught its full impact on the bridge of her nose and on her chin. Dove, following her up the stairs, witnessed the misstep and took over immediately. To stop the bleeding, she had the girl sit up, rather than lie back, and pinch her nostrils together tightly for three minutes, the time it takes healthy blood to clot. Let's ask a teacher about having a dentist look at your teeth, okay? They are probably okay but better safe than sorry."

This incident was a microcosm of Dove's future nursing career. She loved caring for patients, she thought well under pressure, and she was often in the right place at the right time.

Dove graduated third in her class and was offered work as a floor nurse in all five of the hospitals she applied to. She said to each hospital separately:

"I would love to work for you, but I want to do emergency medicine. Can you possibly find a place for me in the Accident an Emergency Department? (Most big hospitals had an A & E section which was the predecessor of the Emergency Room.)

Each hospital, with the exception of Presbyterian said this was not possible, that new RN's had to develop their skills on a general medicine floor for two years before they could be considered for a transfer elsewhere. "Standard policy," they all

97

sang in unison. Presbyterian Hospital, however, gave Dove a fifteen-minute appointment with its Assistant Director of Nursing. Nurse Irons was her name and it was appropriate. She was a stern-faced, iron-willed grey-haired woman with a ferocious reputation for being rigid.

Dove called me the night before her interview. She had figured out her strategy, which sounded fine to me. All she needed was a pep talk, which I could give her, and did. "Thanks, Lottie. I'll send you a note tomorrow to tell you how I did," she said just before hanging up.

"Don't be silly," I shot back. "I could never last that long. Call me."

Nurse Irons was no doubt used to talking more than listening during meetings with nursing students and she was probably not used to hardcore salary negotiating with the young girls who sat across from her. Finally, she couldn't have known that Dove had learned to negotiate at the knee of a highly persuasive attorney. Dove certainly had the element of surprise in her corner as Nurse Irons entered the hospital's wood-paneled conference room. She gave Dove an almost imperceptible nod and seated herself at the head of a beautiful, polished mahogany conference table. She did not offer Dove a chair nor did she gesture that she be seated too. Dove considered this rude, but she had been taught by her father that if someone insults you, strike back with something clever, but not offensive. Dove waited for a moment then sat down uninvited.

"I must tell you that I am not in agreement with the message I bring you this morning," the Assistant Director said. "I think if we reward prima donnas who come here demanding special privileges, it will undermine the discipline we have worked so hard to build here over many years. You wish to work in A & E after learning the basics of nursing on a General Medicine floor for only six months. Am I right? While others have to put in a minimum of two years before moving on. Is that correct?" Our admissions committee voted to make you an exception: that you work in General Medicine for only six months before moving on to A & E. No, I mean one year on the floor, and that your charge nurse approve of your transfer at that time. What do you say?"

Dove picked up two potential clues to Nurse Irons' negotiating position. First, she heard "Admissions Committee voted ..." This probably meant that Nurse Irons was carrying the Committee's final offer, not her own. Second, Dove guessed that Nurse Irons threw in her "one year" offer as a last-ditch effort to force her to conform to the hospital's protocol. If Dove accepted it, the committee wouldn't object. If she rejected the one-year offer, Nurse Irons could have stepped back and done the committee's bidding. As a safety net, Dove was sure that any of the hospitals who had wanted her but insisted that she first work on a general medicine floor would still accept her. Having considered all those variables, she was ready to place her bet.

Increasing her soft Georgia drawl ever so slightly, Dove answered, "Well, I am terribly disappointed, but thank you, Nurse Irons, for taking the time to see me today. I was so hoping to have the opportunity to work for you. My father's best friend, a physician here in the city, made some calls last week and told me I wouldn't be able to find a fairer or kinder nurse to work for in the city than you. I just find it difficult to believe we are arguing over 180 little days when, if all had gone as we both hoped, I might have worked here for well over 7,000 days."

"Where are your numbers coming from, Nurse Colombé? I mean I don't get the 180 and the 7,000." Because Nurse Irons seemed to be interested in Dove's figures, Dove sensed a glimmer of hope.

"The 180 is the six-month offer the Admissions Committee made and which you mentioned just a minute ago. If that's your offer, I gratefully accept. If you are suggesting I spend one year here before being eligible for the ER, then regretfully I will have to go elsewhere."

"And the 7,000 days?" Nurse Irons reminded Dove.

"My multiplication may be off, but I think if I had a twenty-year career here, I'd work close to 7,500 days." Nurse Irons calculated furiously with her paper and pencil. When she finished, she rose quickly and without looking at Dove said, "Be in my office at 7 a.m. Monday. You've got the job, with ER eligibility starting in six months."

As promised, Dove called me that evening and we each opened a bottle of beer and drank them together in celebration of her first job.

Dove was a natural. She learned quickly, worked hard, and maintained excellent relations with her co-workers and superiors. When her case load permitted, she also attended the weekly in-house lectures given by visiting doctors for the staff physicians and other caregivers. Attending these talks raised her profile, increased her contacts and her knowledge of the most common diseases the hospital was treating, such as diphtheria, tetanus, and the various influenzas.

For eight years, Dove labored in Presbyterian Hospital's emergency room, one of the country's busiest and best. Nurse Irons, of all people, recognized her remarkable assessment skills and devotion to her profession by sending her to numerous courses in trauma management, and by supporting her promotion to charge nurse in the ER when she was only 28 years old. This made her the youngest nurse in Presbyterian's history to be given that responsibility.

In the meantime, back in Atlanta, after only a year, I was promoted from gopher to news photographer. I made friends with the reporters and never complained when they called me at night to the scene of a murder or fire or some newsworthy event for which they needed "art." I even won first place in a photo contest for anyone who wanted to enter and an Honorable Mention in a contest for professional photographers only. Dove and I kept up through letters and two phone calls apiece per month.

Arthur, having to know his little girl was safe and comfortable, bought an apartment near the hospital as an investment. He let Dove stay there for a nominal fee. Several times she suggested I come to New York, live with her and try to make it in the big time. Gradually the idea grew on me. I called Dove one night because I'd spotted an ad in a trade journal that looked like I might qualify. "Go for it," she whooped. I sent them my ten best shots, interviewed two men in one call, got the job and moved to the city.

We both worked very hard. Sometimes we didn't see each

other for a week or more, but we were glad to be together because the city could be very lonely. One fix for that problem would have been two good-looking men. We each did go out from time to time, but we were so tired that most of the time an empty bed looked more inviting than a half-full one. Also, looking back on those years, I think we were both driven to prove we were not stupid southerners and/or that most southerners weren't stupid. To do that, perhaps we worked harder than our northern peers. I'm sure Dove would have become an outstanding nurse even if she had stayed in Savannah but working in the Presbyterian Hospital ER allowed her to get there faster. As for me, I found two ways to give myself a small advantage. First, I got the best camera possible, despite the cost. Second, I persuaded my friend Ken Barnett, who had studied electrical engineering at NYU, to soup up my new camera. After a couple of late nights, he had increased the speed with which my flash attachment would recharge, thereby enabling me to take three or more pictures while my competitors were taking one.

I felt indebted to Ken for his work and I liked him as a person. He was smart and cute, and, for good measure, he was even Italian. But, alas, it was not to be. He needed his sleep and I needed my early morning calls from reporters. Our conflicting professional demands clashed once too often, and Kenny was gone.

As Dove and I plied our trades, the countries of Europe were marching directly towards a war no one imagined would be the deadliest in human history. On 28 July 1914, the Archduke Franz Ferdinand and his wife Sophie were in Sarajevo to inspect the imperial armed forces and to celebrate their wedding anniversary. That morning, while riding in an open Graf & Stift touring car with little security, a Serbian terrorist threw a bomb at the archduke. No one in the Archduke's immediate party was seriously hurt, but the bomb did bounce off his car and hit an officer and some bystanders. That afternoon the couple insisted on being driven to the hospital to visit the injured officer. Along the way, again with little security, the driver took a wrong turn. Instantly, he found himself off the road, surrounded by curious onlookers, and unable to move the car in any direction due to the crush of people around him. By chance, a nineteen-year-old Serbian terrorist by the name of Gavrilo Princip who had come to Sarajevo to kill the Archduke, was standing close to the spot where the Archduke's procession had ground to a halt. Recognizing his opportunity, he ran to the touring car and shot the Archduke in the carotid artery and his wife in the abdomen. Both died later that day. Immediately Austria-Hungary and Germany, its ally, declared war on Serbia and its allies, and World War I had begun just as Arthur said it would.

As she read about the assassinations, Dove thought about her father and shook her head in admiration. Seven years ago, Arthur had predicted that some insignificant event – such as a wrong turn, perhaps? – would produce the spark that could ignite a political powder keg – the Balkans? – which would plunge the world into war. He also said that once the powder keg exploded, a shooting war would follow close behind. Those predictions also were already coming true. The Battle of Liege, the first battle of the war was already being contested, and war was being declared by many belligerents.

Dove followed news of the war as closely as possible. She had come home for her birthday in the spring of 1916 and was lying on the living room floor reading *The New York Times*.

"Mother," she shouted into the kitchen, "Have you heard of the Battle of the Somme?"

"No, I don't think so," her mother answered.

"Well, it's been raging for ten days," she yelled. "Guess how many were killed on the first day of fighting. Thirty-one thousand! That's so STUPID," she shouted. "Think of it. It's like if every living soul in our little town were murdered today. And those figures are just for the first day of one battle!"

Dove stopped yelling at her mother. Like most people living in America, Genevieve wasn't worried about the slaughter taking place overseas. So as long as it didn't touch her or her loved ones, her eyes were on her boutique.

But Dove couldn't ignore the war and was beginning to feel restless in New York. She had lived there for nearly a decade. Occasionally, an American Red Cross (ARC) nurse would wander into her ER and they would talk about the war, which the U.S. was not participating in yet. One day after a night shift, Dove walked by the ARC recruiting office on 6th Avenue. The office was not open yet, but the woman inside saw Dove's uniform and opened the door for her.

"May I do something for you?" asked the woman.

"I thought I might pick up some brochures and ask some questions. Should I come back later when you're open?"

"Heavens no. I'm here and ready to go, but we'll shut the door, so others won't come in until we're officially here."

Her name was Margaret Kemper. She was dressed in a shimmering white, starched and ironed ARC nurse's uniform. She listened to Dove casually recite her *curriculum vitae,* but when she said she worked at Presbyterian's ER, Margaret's ears perked up.

"For how long have you worked there?" Margaret asked.

"About eight years," Dove replied. "I'm a charge nurse there."

"Gosh!" Margaret gushed. "How old are you, if you don't mind my asking."

"I'm 28."

"You must be quite a nurse, or else your father owns the hospital. That's a joke, my dear. Presbyterian ... then you must know Nurse Irons."

"Oh, doesn't everyone? She and I got off to a rocky start, but she has taught me so much, given me so many opportunities. She is by far the greatest influence on my nursing career of everybody."

Being appropriately impressed with Dove's credentials, Margaret became more candid with her knowledge of who and what the ARC was hoping to recruit. "You fit our two highest priorities, which are all but mutually exclusive. They are youth and experience. We want both in the same person. And, Dove, that is you. Your skills in trauma care and experience as a supervisor are icing on the cake. You have hit the jackpot. Now all you have to do is negotiate yourself a good contract. I'd shoot high if I were you."

"Thanks, Margaret. I'll have to ponder this, but why did you mention my age as an advantage a minute ago? I would have thought it would be a disadvantage."

"No, my dear. You'd be working in a serious war zone. Sleep is at a premium, food's not great, when you have it, and there is stress always. Fighting wars is not for the elderly."

At that point, three years into the war, the ARC was putting about fifty mobile hospitals and Casualty Clearing Centers into service along the Western Front. The Director of Nursing, stationed in London, oversaw these medical outposts. There were ten deputy Directors of Nursing, each of whom had supervisory responsibility over five or six hospitals. Each hospital had a Chief of Nursing, who ran the hospital, and a Chief of Medicine, a physician who oversaw all things medical. By the time Dove had cleared two interviews, she had set her sights on one of the Chief of Nursing jobs, but to her surprise, the ARC selection committee was thinking she would be better suited to a deputy's job. When all was said and done, the committee offered her what she wanted, but with the understanding that she would move up in six months if both Dove and her supervisor agreed. The ARC gave her three weeks to put her affairs in order and report to the boat in New York.

During the four weeks or so it took Dove and me to decide to go to Europe, we talked about the pros and cons incessantly. We learned that Nurse Kemper was looking for support personnel as well as nurses. She said she would do her darnedest to get us assigned to the same hospital. After covering every possible pro and con many times, we both signed up. I put my name on the paper not so much because Dove was going, although that was a consideration, but because I wanted to be a war photographer. I thought that if I could get one or two really memorable shots, it would go a long way to landing a job with a first-rate newspaper after the war. Signing up with the ARC was the only way I knew to get close to the action, to be a modern-day Mathew Brady. I had had many conversations with vets who had come home from the war and gravitated to the news business. Most of them were of the opinion that there had been too few photographers in theater. My fingers were crossed that I had found a productive niche.

We took the train home to Savannah to tell our parents

what we had done and that we had three weeks to pack and say goodbye. Dove waited until the family had finished its first dinner together to make her announcement.

"Hey, I have something to tell you, something important," she said in an unnatural voice.

Her sister Belle shot back, "You've found a man?"

Then her father said, "Shh, honey, this is important."

Dove ignored them. The first few times she had raised this possibility, during two phone calls and once during Easter vacation, both her parents had been apoplectic. Her struggle to win them over began to feel as entrenched as the war itself. But at that moment before Dove had said anything else, they both seemed to know what she was going to say. Dread strained the familiar features of their faces.

"I am going to be in charge of an entire hospital," she said cheerfully.

"Where is it?" her father asked.

"In Auberny," she answered.

"Is that along the Western Front?"

"Yes, it is, Papa."

"How close to the fighting?"

"About five miles. The longer it takes a wounded man to get to us, the smaller are his chances of survival."

"Yes, I know that," he replied in a whisper. Her father put his head in his hands and looked down on his empty dessert dish. "I'm not mad at you, Honey, but this is so difficult to bear ... that I have to be by myself for a while." He looked as if he were going to cry as he walked out of the room.

His wife followed him dutifully and whispered to Dove, "*Ca va aller, ma Chérie*. It'll be okay, my love."

Dove remembered them looking older as they left the room than they had when they entered. They put on brave faces for the remainder of her days in Savannah, but for the first time Dove had an inkling of how hard her time in France was going to be on Arthur. And in a flash, she had her answer to why he had been so opposed to discussing the idea of his little girl's becoming a nurse: he feared deeply for her life.

I put my parents through a similar ordeal, but our conversation was interrupted constantly by my brothers' and sisters' needs for adjudication, help finding things, asking permission to go out, and a thousand other means of seeking their attention. I wasn't sure whether those distractions made my decision easier for my parents to accept or whether it just seemed easier to me because the atmosphere in the living room made it impossible to say much about it. Before I went to bed that night, both parents told me they were proud of me. They had never said that to me before.

Dove's three weeks flew by, but even if they had given her three years to prepare for what she was to face when she arrived, it wouldn't have been enough time. She landed in Auberny, France, just as the Third Battle of Ypres began. This battle raged and sputtered between July and November and resulted in 300,000 Allied soldiers – mostly French and Belgian – and 200,000 German troops being killed or wounded. Her hospital was overrun twice, not by Germans, but by wounded Allied soldiers. They came in cars, on foot, in buses, on cows and horses, and on bicycles, and some even hitch-hiked. They came until there was no space on the floors for anyone else to lie down.

The medical staff did what it could with insufficient medicines and supplies. Despite their efforts, the death toll rose. Infected wounds, mustard gas burns, typhoid, influenzas, dysentery, and pneumonia were the major killers. Living outside for months on end in close proximity to lice, rats, cadavers, nerve gas, and other filth and poisons, the boys didn't stand a chance; infections were inevitable. Other combatants had the shakes, could not speak or sleep or see. Still others were battling various kinds of paralysis. The diagnosis given to soldiers with these psychologically induced symptoms was "shell shocked."

In addition to all these problems, combatants and caregivers alike had to deal with the effects of chlorine gas, one of the worst of the so-called "industrial weapons" making its debut in the Great War. The Germans pumped the gas from its canisters, making certain the wind was at their backs. As it drifted toward Allied lines, it became an eerie green, strange-smelling vapor. If the doughboys panicked and ran, German machine gunners mowed them down. If they inhaled it, they came down with gas gangrene, the effects of which were horrifying. Nitrogen formed gas bubbles under the skin and gave off crackly noises as the bubbles popped. As the gas entered the bloodstream, the skin turned black and produced enormous quantities of pus. While dressings could be changed and antiseptics used, often the best bet to save a man's life was amputation, but the surgeons had to act quickly and cut high enough above the quickly advancing gangrene to save the infected appendage.

The Third Battle of Ypres turned out wounded soldiers by the thousands, many of whom found Dove's hospital. They came in unannounced, found a piece of floor, lay down and fell asleep, either because they were exhausted from fighting, feinting from blood loss, and countless other wounds. In those first chaotic and supremely sad days, Dove found herself not running a hospital, so much as a triage center. If a patient had a chest wound, Dove would work long and hard to send him not just to another hospital with a bed, but to a hospital with a chest cracker on board. This was, sadly enough, her work and a Herculean change that saved many lives and won Dove her first medal.

During Dove's first 15-20 days, exhaustion became a problem for everyone, especially the surgeons whose skills and judgment were connected most directly to the lives and deaths of their patients. One of their most brutal responsibilities was to write their post-operation reports, in which they were required to explain in their own words what had caused their patients' deaths. Living life under such pressure caused strong men and women to crumble. Depression often with hallucinations became a frequent diagnosis. Little worries became big, irrational ones and personal animosities over petty things became slug fests occasionally. For the most part, however, we got along well with our colleagues in the medical services, despite the fact that our quarters were next to the carpenter's shop. This meant that day and night we had to listen to the tap-tap of their tools as they made their simple, rickety coffins. They built them as fast as they could, but without a prayer they would ever catch up with the demand.

For the troops there were many hurry-up-and-wait days. They provided precious time for rest and the healing of minor injuries. The troops would doze in the afternoon sun, write letters, clean weapons, or shoot the breeze with friends. There were many such days, but there weren't many entertainment days. In fact, that lazy afternoon in early September may have been the only entertainment day of the war.

The noise began without warning and with a distant whine. Within seconds everyone had their hands over their ears to keep this high-pitched, piercing noise from boring into their brains. We soon saw that the sound was emanating from a single Sopwith Camel. The pilot must have kept the rpm's low and hopped some hedges to sneak up on the hospital. Once there, he had taxied a minimal distance, pulled back on the stick and slammed the throttle full forward, thus launching the aircraft on an almost vertical take-off. The closer the little plane came to a vertical climb, the slower it went, the louder it screamed, and the more likely it seemed that it would lose its fight with gravity, stall and fall backwards through the hospital roof. But the reliable Bentley engine prevailed. It pushed the aircraft's nose one, two, three degrees over the peak of the loop. Then, with the pilot hanging upside down in his straps and the plane rapidly gaining speed, it plummeted back down toward Earth. *Seventy-five mph, 90, 110, 130 …* The audience looked away, hearts in their throats, not wishing to watch a young man lose his life before their eyes. Again, the pilot and plane prevailed, pulling out of their power dive with *300 feet to spare*. The pilot then did a couple of rolls – probably to give himself some time to get his breathing back to normal – and landed his plane light as a sparrow close to a gaggle of nurses.

"Anyone want to fly away with me?" he asked only half-jokingly.

Dove had landed at Auberny three weeks earlier than I. Nurse Kemper said I could not travel without my ARC ID card. These cards were effectively our passports, so they were difficult to replace when lost. Finally, it came through with the paperwork for my Military Occupational Specialty. I learned not only that I could depart immediately for my post on the

Western Front, but also that I was to be an Administrative officer. I was to be in charge of whatever Dove asked me to do. Nurse Kemper had come through for us.

When I walked into Dove's small office for the first time, she looked near collapse. Her skin was sagging and had little color. She stooped, even when she was seated. Since we had last seen each other she had lost twelve pounds. I scolded her for not taking better care of herself, but she blamed the influx of patients from the raging Battle of Ypres.

"When we are full to capacity, we have one hundred patients," she explained. "Our high-water mark during the worst of Ypres was 237. Imagine that!"

Then she turned her attention to me and said, "My dear Lottie, welcome. I'm so glad you're here. I'm going to give you only one job, and that'll be running the hospital. You'll be the only clerk in the ARC whose title will be 'executive director' and I would suggest you use it, the title that is, and frequently if necessary. There are lots of nurses here with much experience in hospitals. That doesn't mean they know how to run one. They don't, actually, and the faster you make them understand that, the easier your life will be."

"Maybe I should join their side I don't know how to run one either," I said.

"Lottie, you have more brain power and savvy than everybody in this hospital put together. And, I didn't mean to imply that you would be running the hospital alone. I'll be helping you, and vice-versa, and I'll back you on everything you do. I think both of us would have more weight to throw around if we do not divulge that we have known each other for a long time, probably around 91.2 percent of our lives. Actually, there is another aspect to your job. It has to do with photography, and I'll explain it to you in due course. It's private. For now, I just want you to start taking photos of everything within range, from A to Z. I'll pay all your expenses, including film. Keep a good record of each photo you take and be as discreet as you can."

Dove's face turned serious as she said, "Let me tell you what I tell each nurse when I meet her for the first time. I say, 'By the end of this day you are going to want to leave this goddamned place more than you've ever wanted anything and, I'm sorry to say, that feeling will be with you for a while. You should not feel weak or unqualified if you cry yourself to sleep for the first week or two because many of the women here have.' I usually pause about here to let the message sink in, which is not easy to do. At the end of my talk, I say 'I'm sorry to tell you this, but I know it will help you contend with the problem. You'll feel this way because your nurses will be confronting over and over the most wrenching moment in medicine: the moment you realize you can no longer do anything for your patient. This is a critical moment in their lives, and in yours too. The nurse has got to sit with her patient, hold his hand, give him permission to let go and promise you will stay with him to the end. Remember, they are sacrificing their lives while you are thinking, 'what else should I have done for him … if only I could have … so, you must be compassionate with your patients and gentle on yourselves. Otherwise, you won't last here."

We had talked many times about where my occupation might lead, but I didn't want to bother Dove with that now. She would mention her reasons for asking me to photograph everything photo-worthy when she was ready. In the meantime, it gave me carte blanche to go anywhere I could to shoot photos. What more could I have asked? As time crept along, we developed a routine of meeting every seven to ten days to review the photos I had taken.

So, those were my two jobs: find ways to make the hospital run better and take photographs. All in all, if we'd had better food and no armed Germans living nearby who wanted to kill us, it wouldn't have been a bad job.

Dove had her own philosophy of nursing which gradually became apparent as I worked with her. She believed, and asked her nurses to believe, that good nursing is an attitude, not a subject to be learned from books. "Despite all the straight medical issues you learned about in school, working here on the Front you will confront as many psychological problems as you will medical dilemmas. There are no book solutions for many of the mental problems we see because the weapons we face are new to combat and inflict such heinous wounds that we don't yet know the best ways to treat them."

Dove used to say, "Anyone can learn to tie a tourniquet or clean and dress a wound, but who knows how to treat a 20-year-old man, who wanted to be an artist, and is now blind? My answer: a good nurse who follows her instincts and teaches her patients to be persistent will figure out how to treat him. The doctors aren't going to involve themselves in their patients' morale and employment problems. They don't have time. So, it's up to you, girls," she insisted. "You work in a life and death business, which is a privilege and a burden because with it you have the responsibility to fight like hell for every single life you touch." Exhausted though I was, I had no trouble getting out of bed in the morning because I knew we were going to make a difference in the lives of our boys, even the ones who would die in our arms.

"You will be living close to these nurses," Dove told me. "Almost all are experienced, dedicated women. Nonetheless, this is the hardest job any of them has ever had because we lose so many patients. That's why I want you to understand what they are going through almost every day. When you see something special, tell the nurse how much you admire her. They can use all the encouragement we can deliver to them. Occasionally you may be able to help with a patient. Always check with the patient's nurse first. Some nurses appreciate help, others are very possessive of their patients and wouldn't think of surrendering the responsibility of treating their wounds to anyone else. Part of your job is to nurse the nurses and to let them know how important their job is. You will realize soon that it is the nurses' skills, not mine, that hold this place together. So anytime you and I and others have a meeting scheduled and a nurse calls and says, 'I can't come I'm too busy,' take her at her word. She will be right 90% of the time."

"Do you really mean that?"

She nodded and I stood, sensing her briefing was over.

Dove stood too then and made a little pronouncement: "You understand the importance of our task. You're tough as tripe and you'll be fine. And let me tell you, my oldest and dearest friend," she said reaching out to take me in her arms, "now that you're here I know we will be able to do what is expected of us."

Since the hospital was overwhelmed with wounded when Dove arrived, she played the role of utility infielder for four days in a row without taking a break. I arrived three weeks after Dove and did the same thing – anything and everything. Occasionally, Dove would think of her supervisor, Nurse Helen Leach. *We must call her*, Dove said to me several times. I finally got around to it on day ten.

When someone with Nurse Leach handed her the phone, she answered, "Hello?"

"Nurse Colombé will be right with you," I replied in my most official yet welcoming voice. "She's removing a suture from an eyelid at this moment. Just a minute, please."

Dove took the phone from my hand about 30 seconds later and said, "Sorry Nurse Leach ..." but she had already hung up and the line was dead.

"We're off to a bad start with the new boss," she said with a shrug.

Dove got her again ten minutes later and Nurse Leach's first words were, "I wish you had phoned me earlier. I've been wondering about you."

"Wondering?" Dove replied in a weak voice. "Not worried or concerned?" With these words Dove's eyes rolled up in her head and she reached for me as she fell.

During the proceeding seven days Dove had not met the minimum requirements for food, water, or sleep. She knew she was dehydrated, had numbness in both hands and both feet and was dizzy. Dr. Ron "Dead Pan" Hurley, Chief of Medicine, was at her side as she was carried to a rest tent. He gave her an IV and a sedative and she slept for 14 hours. His diagnoses: dehydration and exhaustion. Nurse Leach did not try to phone Dove again that day. Instead, she left word that she would be down to see Dove the following week.

'Dead Pan' Hurley advised Dove not to bring up the incident when Nurse Leach came to visit. "Everybody already knows what happened, Dovie, and most office etiquette experts agree," he reasoned with a straight face, "that those who shit on their new supervisors during their first

112

encounters often have difficulty establishing good relationships with those supervisors."

Being a new guy on the block, Dove didn't have a good network to tell her how best to deal with Nurse Leach. Dove, of course, wanted to squeeze out all the practical information possible out of her, but some folks don't accumulate – or even hear – that kind of information. When they finally shook hands, Dove knew within thirty seconds that Nurse Leach was going to be difficult.

Dove asked that all nurses who weren't working to convene in the mess tent, a venue often used for meetings. Dove gave a short introduction and handed the meeting over to Nurse Leach, who plowed into a long monologue on why rules are important when people are working in difficult circumstances. Hardly pausing for breath, Nurse Leech began another cliché-riddled speech on how to chart better. For example," droned Leach, "I expect you to take the Death Count first thing each morning before doing anything else and be sure the COD – Cause of Death – is specific. In short, the COD should never read 'heart failure' because that is not informative. Everyone's heart fails when they die," Nurse Leach said. Dove felt embarrassed and guilty for having set her nurses up for this childish talk and waste of time.

"Okay, girls, how about question time?" Nurse Leach, after an hour and a half, was acting kittenish! "I couldn't have answered all your questions, could I?" she asked in a sing-song delivery perfect for kindergarten. In this situation, there is always one question asker. She raises her hand a millisecond before the speaker starts to say her goodbyes. She opens her mouth to ask a question but talks in circles listening to her own voice. This, in turn, produces a groan from the audience that gathers above them like a dark cloud. But these nurses are highly efficient, no nonsense, workers whose minds are always at least half on their patients. They had heard enough. Not one of them said a word or moved a muscle. Mrs. Leach tried to outwait them, but finally she said thank you and goodbye, the only thing she had done proficiently since she arrived.

Dove sat with Nurse Leach in the Motor Pool while she

113

waited for her convoy of trucks and jeeps to form up. Nurse Leach was going to Ypres, the last hospital on her present tour. . It was a long, awkward wait for Dove, knowing the visit had not gone well for her and assuming it had not gone well for 'the Leach,' as the girls had taken to calling her, either. In saying goodbye, Dove tried to shake her hand warmly and said, "Next time I'll arrange for you to have some private time with some of the girls. They work so hard and still manage to be kind and smile ..."

Nurse Leach cut her off saying, "Next time we'll meet at my place. I have a long, dangerous ride home now."

Nurse Leach was seated in the back of Vehicle #6, a jeep, with a corpsman. A major was riding shotgun with an M-3 rifle, not much protection. They set off about thirty minutes before sundown, later than usual. The attack occurred about twenty minutes outside of Ypres. The driver was first to see the machine gun tracers flying at them but well over head. As the Germans adjusted their fire down, the jeep driver lost control of his vehicle and it plunged into a ditch. At that point, Nurse Leach was lying ten yards away from the driver, face down in a mud puddle. She would have suffocated there had the driver not crawled to her, despite a broken leg, a collapsed lung, and the last of the enemy fire landing around him and yanked her head out of the sticky mud. The driver and corpsman survived. The major perished; he had broken his neck when the jeep careened off the road. The Germans disappeared into the night.

Dove offered to write the death notification letter and spent much more time on it than she usually did. As she struggled to write the major's parents, she thought of Arthur and how devastated he would be if someone had to write a letter like that for Dove sometime. She remembered how weak and small he looked that last time she saw him. But, as usual, the question that haunted her most was, why did the major have to die?' By now she knew the answer: there was none. Death during war was almost always random. How she hated that answer. It seemed to draw all the nobility – the sacrifice, the heroism, the selflessness – out of a soldier's death. The only explanation a proud parent could give for his son's death in battle had become: 'somebody's got to do it.'

At the end of her first month, Dove called an all-hands meeting. "Ladies," she began, "we have some matters to discuss, but first I wish to tell you, having watched you during our three two weeks of Hell, that I am very proud to be among you. You are an inspiration and I will never forget you. I hope in time I'll be able to call myself one of you."

The tent was absolutely quiet. All of the staff members were immediately aware that this was not the usual old school Chief of Nursing. This was the new guard speaking. Dove knew some would prefer to stay with the old-school rules and routines. She hoped others would prefer the new-school ways. Be that as it may, Dove had decided to be herself, to take another chance.

"Please raise your hand if you think you know when your patients are close to death," she asked. Most of the women raised their hands. "In my opinion, the moment you know you can no longer help your patient is the very moment you *must* try your hardest to connect with him, to communicate with him, even if you don't know he's communicating with you. Comfort him in his final moment. Give him permission to *let go*. Hold his hand if that gives him comfort. Sit close to him if he's cold. Remember, these men have given everything they have to win this war. In return, we must summon every bit of skill and every ounce of compassion we possess to keep them alive and to make them strong again so they can go home and hug their parents and play with their children. We of all people on earth know how precious and fleeting life is. Let us never surrender it."

"The last matter: I am going to work with you two days a week. One on the floor, one in OR. I would like to work even more as a real nurse, but time will tell. I know my predecessor did not do this, but I believe that to understand your problems and to help you find solutions I must spend time with the real workforce. Also, I have some skills that will allow me to save the surgeons time, especially when we are overbooked, and I want to preserve those skills and add a few more. That is all, Ladies. I thank you for coming."

Dove turned and walked out of the tent. I met her at the

exit flap and walked with her to our office. The nurses stood but curiously they did not head directly for the exit flaps. There was a moment of uncertainty and then some scattered clapping. Then more. Finally, full-bodied applause broke out. It lasted a full minute. Dove heard it, but she did not break stride. When she reached her office, she flopped into the chair behind her desk and allowed a big smile to light up her face.

"Well, whadaya think, Lottie?"

"Bask in it, Chief, but the fight ain't over yet."

It was her first happy moment at Auberny.

Dove wrote a letter to her parents that afternoon and asked me to read it like the censors would. It went like this:

"I have been here three months and feel I'm beginning to get a grip on the job. The majority of nurses here are American and British and they know their stuff. As a result, I see myself more as their cheerleader than their coach. But the nurses on the floor invest so much of themselves in their patients and lose so many of them – through no fault of their own – that the girls are susceptible to exhaustion and depression. I try to watch over my flock – I have 75 now – and get involved if their closest friends, the nurses they work with every day, cannot pull them out of their doldrums. In those cases, if I fail too, a regimental psychiatrist can be called in. There are many degrees to the nurses' psychological problems and many solutions. Some girls work out their problems quickly by themselves. Others have to be sent home."

Although Dove was clearly in charge of her hospital by the end of her third month, she had not picked up rumors that a group of older conservative nurses were opposing her orders to be physically comforting to their dying patients if holding a hand or sitting with them seemed to quiet them.

Dove believed in hands-on care because she had seen its results over and over in the ER in New York. Surprising outcomes always made her think of Mr. Livingston, a tough, old West Virginia farmer who had ridden up San Juan Hill with Teddy Roosevelt and had recently suffered a heart attack while visiting his daughter in Washington. Ten days after his admission, he had deteriorated to the point that the chief cardiologist told Dove to *hang crepe* with the family and friends because he had little time remaining. Two days later Mrs. Livingston arrived at the hospital worried and angry. The hospital had assumed the daughter had been apprising her mother of Mr. Livingston's condition and the daughter had assumed the hospital had. Let us just say communication had been poor on everyone's side.

Rather than become ensnarled in a he-did-she-did argument, Mrs. Livingston stuck her head in the nurses' room and said, 'Where's Livingston's room?'"

When she arrived, Mr. Livingston appeared to be asleep. Mrs. Livingston must have had a commanding presence because all three staff members left the room quickly after she entered. The nursing staff could see the Livingstons through a large window separating Mr. Livingston's private room from the ward, but they could not hear them. Mrs. Livingston sat on her husband's bed, held his hand, and began to speak. Fifteen seconds or so later, he opened his eyes, and in another fifteen, he smiled and produced two tears that ran from the corner of his eye to his ear. "The Mrs.," as he referred to his wife, spoke for about two minutes and ten days later Mr. Livingston was discharged to home where he worked as hard as he did before the war for another five years. As he was leaving, when one of the staff asked him what "the Mrs." had said that turned his status from hopeless to reasonably healthy, he said, "It wasn't no big deal. She jist tole me that she loved me but weren't anywhere near ready to die right yet, but she knew she would die if she had to live without me. So, she said, 'I *ain't askin'* you to do nothing I wouldn't do for you if the situation was reversed. I'm *jist askin'* you to *git* better and come home to me because I need you! So, as usual, I did what she said."

Most doctors and nurses have seen examples of love's power to heal, but a contingent of nurses, led by Nurse Leach, apparently saw holding hands as a means of stimulating a dying soldier's libido or sitting on his bedside to discuss end-of-life issues as a way of increasing his potential for licentious behavior. I suppose these conservative women felt betrayed when Dove changed the rules. To retaliate, they wanted to make Dove look bad so the authorities would throw her out. They were talking about starting a rumor campaign that would spread the word that Dove had been a barroom dancer, that she had had several children out of wedlock, and that she drank liquor secretly at night.

I'm proud to say I'm the one who uncovered this budding revolt. I slept in the gym when I first arrived and, by chance, I heard those three nurses discussing ways to undermine Dove. They mentioned Nurse Leach frequently as if she were the mastermind behind this effort. The following night I went to bed early, but fell asleep, not knowing what, if anything, I had missed. The third night they said they were sure they would be able to "fix Dove's wagon." There was considerable giggling and whispering, but I could feel their excitement even through my blanket which I had pulled up over my face.

As soon as I got to our tent the next morning, I told Dove what I had heard. She listened attentively and then asked, "Can you identify these three women?"

"I don't know how I could do that without risking suspicion, which I'm willing to do if you want me to."

"My answer is don't risk drawing any suspicion to yourself. We don't know what these women are capable of doing. Understood?"

"You've got to be careful too, Dove. I'm not kidding. We're dealing with fundamental religious beliefs here. Religious fanatics are not known for their ability to listen to the other side. Leach can be rough with patients. She might be the same with you."

"What do you mean 'rough with my patients?'" Dove asked. I noticed the important two-letter addition. Now the patients were *hers*.

"I mean she can be impatient with them and impulsive."

"I will not have anyone bullying my patients. How do you know this about her?"

"I was in her ward two days ago and heard her raise her voice to Sgt. Briley. "I have also seen her jerk patients upright in bed by one arm and rebuke them for poor hygiene habits. I can write up the details if you wish."

118

"Yes, do that. Write the memo to me with all the detail you can recall. After I see it, put it in a safe, locked place. Thanks, Lottie. You do good work."

"But what are we going to do about her?"

"Are there other plotters at Leach's level, do you know?"

"My guess is no, there are not. Your first presentation about the change in rules was well received. The girls really liked the idea of staying with the dying until the end."

"Let me think about this for a while. I'll come up with something. In the meantime, I want you to talk to each of the boys you think Leach may have abused or treated harshly and very subtly give them an opportunity to complain about Leach if they wish to. Your purpose will be to determine if they feel they could suffer more injury here in this hospital. *Very subtly* are the key words, okay?"

"Yep," I said.

About that time, the Third Battle of Ypres raised its vicious head yet again and many young men started to die. Dove could not drop all she was doing to run down an apparently small group of insubordinate nurses and their leader. But there was a way. All she had to do was read the charts. If the nurses were charting honestly and accurately about the new care methods for their dying patients, Dove would be able to know who they were simply by reading their charts. So, as time permitted – usually late at night – Dove and I would pore over the nurses' notes, making our own notes on separate sheets of paper. The results had to be considered anecdotal, not scientific, but Dove was pleased to see that out of the seventy-five nurses at her hospital, sixty-six were using – and charting – the newly instituted methods of care.

"So what percentage favors in the new policy, Dove?" I asked as my memory carried me back to our morning walk to school when we calculated that we had known each other for 87.5 percent of our lives. I thought from the look on her face, that she had already figured out the answer.

"Eight-eight percent favor the new directive," she said.

"You're amazing," I replied.

But Dove had seen many signs of the change. Recently, as

she made her rounds, her eye caught the eye of Nurse Adams, one of her favorites, sitting with one of her patients.

"How's it going?" Dove asked.

"He can't talk. Trachea burned by gas," Nurse Adams answered. "But I know he appreciates my being here. No doubt at all."

Another nurse told Dove longingly, "These wonderful boys have given their voices and vision, they've been shot, concussed, poisoned with gas, and they've broken their bones, but as wonderful and heroic as they are," the nurse said facetiously, "I'm afraid none of them will be thinking of sex for at least three or four more days."

Not one nurse complained of being the object of a sexual advance as a result of her showing a little more human compassion and kindness than she had before. With this information and her intuition, Dove was ready to make her move.

As the number of patients from two nearby battlefields filled Dove's 100-bed hospital with almost 275 patients and floor space disappeared under stretcher after stretcher, Dove worked herself into a deep fatigue. She was so tired she couldn't sleep well. She did fall into a dreamless sleep for about 30 minutes while resting her head on her forearm in the cafeteria one morning. When she went to the bathroom to splash some water on her face, she hardly recognized the old, red-eyed woman with the gaunt, pale face staring back at her. "What happened to me?"

The ARC Advisory Board was to meet in London in mid-December. As normal attrition, surgical resolutions, and transfers by hospital trains had dropped Auberny back toward its normal 100-bed capacity and fighting was on the wane as Christmas approached, Dove took another chance and sent a telegram to the Director of Nursing asking permission to come to London to discuss a matter discreetly with her. Dove was surprised to see the Director's response the next morning.

The telegram read: "Nurse Colombé report to ARC Headquarters London earliest convenience. Consider this communication your orders. Peters." The problem came when Dove informed her supervisor, Nurse Leach, by telegram of her impending trip to London. Instantly, Dove received a phone call from Nurse Leach. Leach was incoherent with rage, but she could do nothing to prevent it. It was a *fait accompli.*

Three days later, in London, Dove briefed the Director, Miss Peters, on the situation. She was nervous but delivered her remarks in a matter-of-fact military tone.

"The three rules I propose to change are: nurses will not touch their patients affectionately, such as hold their hands; nurses will not sit on patient's beds; and nurses will not appear in the wards of their patients when they are off duty. For starters, these changes would apply only to our treatment of patients whom we believe are going to die soon. These rules are old-fashioned, prudish, and possibly even detrimental to the recovery of our sickest patients. These changes are experimental and in effect for six months, after which a decision would be made to make them and others permanent or go back to our old ways.

"My decision has provoked a mutiny, I suppose you could call it, which I have learned about through my secretary. By reading the nurses' notes since my meeting with them, I estimate there are sixty-six nurses out of a total of seventy-five, who are practicing and, therefore, favor the new policy. For what it's worth, that's eighty-eight percent favor the new.

"I must be honest and tell you I think there is the possibility of violence in this situation based on the last words I heard from Nurse Leach."

"And what were those words?" the Director asked.

"They were directed at me and they were, 'Don't come back here looking for work, you little bitch. You're finished here.'"

"Looks like you dug yourself a pretty deep hole, young lady," Director Peters said.

"Yes, I'm sorry ..."

"Here's what we are going to do. I will introduce you to the Board at the meeting Wednesday night and you will brief them on what has happened. In the meantime, hone your briefing. Make it more persuasive, less neutral, and less clinical. Draw up a difficult question or two to ask those members who will already have decided to vote no. You've

121

been thinking about this much more than they have. You should be able to persuade at least one or two of the nine to come over to your side. We'll give the Board responsibility for making the final decision because it does go to the core of our care. Any questions?"

"Whose side are you on?"

"I always try to be on the winning side," she said with no trace of a smile.

The final vote was 6 to 3 in favor of allowing the experimental methods to be practiced for six months. The director moved Nurse Leach to Headquarters in London and Dove to Leach's job of overseeing five hospitals and two Casualty Clearing Stations, plus the extra responsibility of writing and promoting the ARC's new transitional policy on care giving. This was a big load, but Dove worked diligently through the winter lull in hostilities trying to fulfill her various responsibilities.

The winter had been especially cold and dreary and the troops on both sides were spent from injuries, illness, deprivation and depression. So, they slept and slept, hibernating through the winter like bears. The average foot soldier, no matter his nationality, complained that his officers would not tell them anything about the future; the food was awful; their feet were always wet and cold at best; and they were constantly being told to hurry up and wait.

But it appeared as if the Earth was still turning as, at long last, spring began to send out its first emissaries. Wild hyacinth, forsythia and lilac appeared during the Meuse-Argonne offensive, in which so much more blood would be spilled right up to Armistice Day. Violets, daffodils, and bluebells decorated the hills and fields all along the 450-mile scar known as the Western Front.

The initial trickle of American troops coming to Europe rose to 200,000 per month and their presence began to be felt on the battlefield. This was a good sign militarily for the Allies, of course, but there would be more death and destruction to come.

On the first day that the nurses could feel real warmth radiating from the sun, six of them grabbed a baguette from the cafeteria, a half bottle of wine from an icebox, and a carton of 'fresh fruit.' They crossed the road in front of the hospital, sat down in the bright green spring grass and spread a sheet out before them. No sooner had they taken that first swallow of wine, than a German artillery battery began to practice. This sound became a harbinger of the last months of the War to End All Wars.

By late September there was serious fighting all along the Western Front between the French-U.S. alliance and the Germans. Despite trying unsuccessfully for three years to break through the German defenses, suddenly the U.S. and France were defeating the Germans, throwing them out of their trenches and bunkers and, on a good day, taking back 1–5 miles of territory. Ironically, this made Dove's job very stressful. Occasionally, some of those Germans who were ousted from their bunkers formed into little bands of leaderless, crazed soldiers marauding the land. Primarily they were looking for food and water, but if women were available, so much the better. The last thing in the world Dove or any of the nurses wanted was to be kidnapped by the Germans. So, I disseminated the following order: "All nurses travelling off the hospital grounds will do so only in groups of five or larger; all nurses will be on hospital grounds between 1700 hours and 0700 hours; for every group of five nurses, a minimum of one will be carrying a sidearm – the more the better." It was perversely fortunate that the fighting and casualties increased. As they did, the nurses found themselves overwhelmed inside their hospital, with less time to be outside.

The fighting continued until Armistice Day, 11 November 1918. During those 47 days of fighting the Battle of the Argonne Forest, the U.S. lost 27,000 men, the French 70,000, and the Germans 100,000.

When the Armistice was signed, Europe was like a one-room schoolhouse filled with students waiting for summer recess to begin. When the headmaster gave the signal, the recess bell rang, and everyone ran for home. Dove did not have the energy to think about returning home. She and I went to London and stayed with Director Peters. One evening after

123

dinner, Director Peters asked if Dove would consider going home on a troop carrier as Head Nurse.

"It would only require that you monitor 10-20 men's conditions once or twice a day," she said.

"Of course, I would, if it would be helpful to you," Dove answered.

"And, Lottie, I arranged a space for you next week," she said handing me an envelope full of tickets and instructions. "And you're welcome to stay here with me until your departure." So, I was facing a one-week vacation in London again and a week's ocean cruise. Life was looking up.

The evening before Dove left for Le Havre, she dashed off a note to her parents. She apparently had some second thoughts after proofreading it because she handed it to me and said, "Do you think the first paragraph is too harsh, too truthful? Does it sound like I'm whining? I don't want to upset them."

She had written:

"It is almost too much for me to realize I will be with you soon. Prepare yourselves. I weigh almost thirty pounds less than I did when I left. I have been away from you for only twenty months, but I have slept so little, worked so hard, cried so often, and suffered so deeply with our wonderful boys that I am no longer the same person.

"While aboard, I will be the Chief Medical Officer, but the work should not be arduous as most of the boys are strong enough to cross the ocean without medical assistance. This will give me one last chance to offer my skills and devotion to our boys who have given so much of themselves."

"I will call you from NYC and come home directly. Love to you both,
Dove

You may call Lottie's folks and tell them she will be home a week to ten day after me."

"It's lovely and straight from the heart. What more could they want?" Lottie said.

At 7 a.m. on our third day at sea there was a knock-on Dove's stateroom door. A formally dressed member of the ship's crew introduced himself and said, "The captain would like to see you in his cabin, Madam. Can you follow me, please?"

"Yes, of course."

Her mind raced through a litany of disasters on which the captain might wish to consult with his chief medical officer, but when he opened his cabin door, the expression on his face alerted Dove to something serious and perhaps personal.

"Please, Dove, sit down." He cleared his throat. "I received a telegram twenty minutes ago and it breaks my heart to have to tell you that your father died at home yesterday apparently of a heart attack. I'm so sorry. You may use the ship's facilities to communicate with your family and friends as often as you wish without charge. If there is anything else I can do for you, all you need do is ask. Would you like a drink?"

Her expression betrayed no emotion as she said, "Yes, please, Captain. Scotch on just a little ice, thank you."

Some weeks later, Dove told me she had put away three healthy scotches and talked about her father for almost three hours. She said she told emotional stories, funny stories, and sad stories about their extraordinary relationship, but she did not shed tear. She told the captain she felt lonely but not sad.

"How could I feel sad when I had the best father in the world? He listened to me. He taught me things. He trusted me." When she left, the captain dispatched his orderly to accompany her to her room for safety's sake. There she passed out for eight hours and when she awoke and realized what had happened, the first tears fell.

Dove felt terribly alone in the middle of the ocean without any friends, but life went on, as did her responsibilities. One of Dove's charges during the Atlantic crossing was Sergeant Pete Rosi, a handsome 25-year-old staff sergeant of Sicilian heritage, whose father had died while his son was serving abroad. Dove knew Pete quite well as he had been admitted to her hospitals on three different occasions, each time with new bullet wounds.

When Dove scolded him for being reckless, Pete said, "Those Krauts can't kill me, Lovie Dovie. You know that down inside, don't you?" He lived as if he really believed that, and maybe he did. Given the chances he took in combat some of the young lads in his platoon believed he was bulletproof. Pete had been itching to get into the war, so he went to England in 1916 and fought voluntarily for the British. Unfortunately, he ended up at the Battle of Verdun where approximately one million men were killed or wounded – but not Pete.

When her ship departed from France, Dove assumed that Pete's recuperative powers would have him on deck competing to catch the first glimpse of lights shining from America's shores. But as the days rolled by Pete evinced little interest in his condition, or anything else. His chart indicated he had a "URI," Upper Respiratory Infection, with recurring fever, but Dove had reservations about that diagnosis. Throughout the crossing, his lung sounds were not bad nor were they worsening. His heart rate was normal for a person who had been outdoors, literally fighting for his life for the past two years. Dove would check his vital signs each morning, then take him up to the top deck where they would go for short walks or just watch the ocean roll by. Pete spoke mostly of his younger brother Ross, his father the surgeon, and his mother, the classical piano player; but the playful sparkle in his eye that Dove had found so endearing was gone.

On the last day of their passage, Pete was not in his ward when Dove made her morning call on him. When he did not appear for lunch, she grabbed an orderly and said, "Stan, I want to see Sgt. Rosi here in ten minutes. Otherwise, it's an all-hands-on-deck drill. Get it?'"

"Got it."

Five minutes later, Stan found Pete in an unused cabin. He was awake but in bed and coughing occasionally. Stan took Dove to him since Pete would not leave his cabin.

"How's your cough, Pete?" she asked.

"Never better," he replied.

"Well, let's get you up on deck to smell that lovely sea air and see the New England coastline."

Pete turned obediently and walked unsteadily toward the stairs. He had trouble climbing the single flight and stepping up and through the frame of a heavy steel door. When Dove opened the door onto the deck, three young men were lounging on a bench right in front of them.

"I wonder if you fellas would let Pete take a turn on the bench" Dove asked. "He's not feeling his best." The boys were off the bench in a flash.

"Get better quick, Gumba," one of them said. "We'll be home soon, buddy. G'day, Miss."

Those boys would not have surrendered that bench to just anyone, but Pete had special status among the troops. He had seen more days of combat than any other; he was the most highly decorated soldier on board; and he had a reputation for always putting his men's safety before his own.

"Oh Hell, Lovie," he had said to her several days earlier, "they've got two more Purple Hearts waiting for me in the Admin Office, but I haven't gone by to pick them up. If you want them, you can have them. They're a gift from me for taking such good care of me."

While he recovered from his walk up the stairs, Dove studied him closely and began to worry. She did not want to upset him, so she gathered her assessment data on his current health status simply by observing and listening. She could see and hear his labored, rapid breathing and he was so thin his heart rate was visible along his carotid artery and it was considerably elevated. His lips were purplish and his skin a pasty greyish color.

Dove had seen more than her share of lungs seared from the inhalation of chlorine gas. Pete's symptoms added up to gas induced lung infection, undoubtedly bilateral. A year ago, he could have dispatched that infection and been back in action a week or two later, but not now.

Pete had been living outside fighting for his life – and the lives of his men – for two years. That green, private first class, who had wandered around the Verdun battlefield upright and aimlessly not knowing that that irritating, whining sound going by his head all the time was the sound of angry bullets that had been shot at him. Finally, a buddy tackled him and suggested he *hunker down* for a while. He didn't know what that meant either. Since that incident, Dove speculated, Pete had watched men deal out so much inhumanity to others that perhaps he had lost faith in his fellow man or, even worse,

127

perhaps in himself. She looked at him, slouched next to her, and put her arm around his shoulder for support. His eyes were closed. He was no longer fully conscious.

"Pete, you can let go now," she said to him. "It's okay. Your father's waiting for you."

Having so little strength, it seemed as if he might just slip forward and slide off the bench. But Dove was with him. She had done this before. She was there when he looked up with unseeing eyes to say goodbye to her and she was holding him close to her when he drew his last breath that brisk afternoon in the late fall of 1918.

~ ~ ~

Approximately seventeen million men gave their lives during World War I. For the rest of Dove's life, the memory of Pete Rosi would stand for those seventeen million patriots. In her mind, he symbolized their loss of innocence. He stood for the guilt they felt at taking a life for the first time and the shame they suffered at discovering the second time was easier. In her mind, Pete also stood for the loss of those millions of ideas, inventions, and creations that died before they were born.

THE BOOK

Dove was bone tired from her year at the Front and from her long, sad trip home. Her overnight train from New York was scheduled to arrive on time in Savannah at 9 a.m. Dove sat staring out of the train window at the boring rural landscape – red clay, evergreens, live oaks and scruffy ground covering – but she saw none of it. She rested her head on the back of her seat and drifted into a shallow slumber.

She was awakened by passengers preparing to get off in Savannah and was fortunate to engage a Redcap porter who hauled her three heavy suitcases and several bags to a taxi and helped the driver strap them to his roof. When Dove tried to tip him, he bowed slightly and said, "Welcome home, Miss Dove."

"Thank you," Dove replied, wondering how the man knew who she was.

Fifteen minutes later her taxi came to a halt in front of Dove's home at 324 Habersham Street. The cabbie carried her luggage onto the porch and then refused a tip. Dove was perplexed at first, then slightly angry.

"I want you to take this tip from me, young man," she said in an authoritative voice. "I'm sure you don't want me to call your company and complain, do you?"

"No Ma'am, Miss Dove," the boy called as he slid into his taxi and drove off. As the sound of the taxi faded into the brisk morning air, she noticed she was shivering – no, she was shaking. She had imagined this moment countless times, but never once without her father. She did tell me one day several months after we had returned that she did see her father that morning. He appeared on the veranda for a few seconds. As his image faded, Pete Rosi's appeared next to his. Dove insisted that a line-up of images of men for whom she had cared, but who had not survived had stood before her to appeal to her that she not forget them. She said the experience was not scary and she was happy that her friends from the war had a chance to meet her father. She was sure they would remain friends. When the last image faded from view, Dove didn't trust her legs to carry her forward toward the house. At that moment she heard Cary's voice.

"Miss Dove, Miss Dove! Oh, Gracious Lordie, you gonna freeze yourself to death. I swear you look so beautiful you must be one of God's very own angels." Cary, a one-woman welcoming committee, continued to talk as she and Dove hugged and hustled Dove into the warm house.

Everything about the house was surreal at first. Reminders of her father almost overwhelmed her. Scents of his pipes and tobaccos and the musty library aroma beckoned to her. It was enticing, but she turned away.

As if she were reading Dove's mind, Cary said, "There's plenty-a-time, Miss Dove. Take it slow."

Dove said later that she felt out of sync with all of her father's possessions and interests, and far removed from the reality of Savannah and her own home. Arthur had seen to it that Genevieve and Maribelle were well taken care of, including a residence each; but the Federalist-style home on Troup Square was Dove's.

After a shower and a light breakfast, Dove tried to sleep, but she couldn't. She padded around in bare feet and marveled that the water rose up dependably every time she pushed the handle on the toilet. She felt the linen table napkins and repeatedly examined the hand-wrought silver salt and pepper shakers. They were beautiful, but who would spend time making dents in silver plate when there were so many important things to be done for so many desperate people? Her first night at home, she slept like the dead, on silk sheets under an English duvet filled with goose down.

At breakfast on the second day, she watched her fresh, cold milk – what she would have given for that six months ago – swirl against the edge of the glass and spill over its lip onto the breakfast table where she and her father had spent time discussing the problems and options that life presented. The memory of talking to him drew her down the hall in a trance to his study. She moved cautiously toward his chair behind his desk as if she sensed danger. And then it escaped, a long, inhuman groan followed by tears, and short desperate sobs.

As if she knew what was going to happen, Cary had remained a discreet distance from Dove, but never out of sight. Before the Dove's moan had ended, she had taken Dove in her arms, like she did when Dove was a little girl, and there she stayed for some time, rocking her and patting her back. When the crying subsided, Cary said quietly, "You take a deep breath now, Dove Honey, and slowly blow it out your mouth." Gradually, Dove relaxed. "Now, we going to walk you upstairs and draw you a warm bath," she said. "You bathe and put on some clean clothes I'll lay out for you, Meanwhile, I'm going to make you some French toast, your favorite."

"Thank you, Cary. I love you; you know. I lost a patient on the boat, dad's room and she shuttered. While preparing for her bath, she saw two letters addressed to her from France, one from her mother explaining she was having difficulty obtaining permission to bring her parents to the U.S. and the other from her sister Belle, asking that Dove call her the minute she arrived.

In the days and weeks that followed, Cary and Belle nursed the nurse. Dove ate three meals a day and took long walks through town, stopping at restaurants and stores where friends worked. Little by little Dove gained weight and energy, and even the desire to reenter civilization. She also learned that Arthur had written regularly columns based on her letters. The articles had a small picture of Dove's smiling face and usually described some detail of the life of a nurse working on the Western Front. The column was popular and made Dove a well-known and admired citizen of their town.

In due course, Dove called me in New York where I was staying with friends. "When are you coming down?" she asked. "I have a nice bedroom for you on the third floor. It's quiet, just like you like it. No machine guns to worry about. You can stay as long as you want."

"I'll buy my ticket and let you know the time and date of my arrival. How are you feeling? Every little ole thing okay?"

"Yeah. Oh, don't forget your pictures. Bring every last one of them, hear?"

"Really? You want all of them? There must be over five thousand."

"Bring them all. I'll tell you all about our next project but I want to do it in person so I can watch your reaction."

131

Shortly after my arrival we were seated on the veranda, which Dove had mentioned so often, both of us with an ice-cold mint julep in hand.

"I would like to write a book about our life on the Western Front," Dove began. "I'd like it to be a *big* book, the kind you would put on the table in front of your sofa. It would be both a collection of photos and a written history of what we did and how we felt about it. The purpose: to enlighten the public about how sickening and agonizing and stupid it is to fight a war. I want to stick our readers' faces right in the messy parts of it. I want them to see what gas gangrene does to one's legs and what a morgue looks like after 30,000 cadavers are shipped to it without orders and what an 18-year-old boy looks like 60 seconds after seeing his buddy take a round in the mouth. For the cover, I want a close up of that young soldier who had just arrived at the hospital after carrying his wounded buddy five miles from the battlefield. Remember that one? His eyes were full of sadness and resignation, but one could also see hope.

"Great, great shot, Lottie. I believe that will become one of the iconic photos of this war. I don't believe we should be one-sided, however. You have lots of shots of the good things too, don't you?' Like the friendships, the bravery, the kindness that occurred so often. Dove was getting excited as she tossed out one idea after another. "What do you think, Lottie? Are you in? There might be some good money in it too."

"I'm ready to sign up right now. I even have a pen ready."

"Well, let's not jump the gun," Dove said. We've got to get Belle established somewhere before I can put my shoulder to the grindstone in this book idea. She's my little sister and I owe her more time and attention than I've given her. Plus, I think she has doubts about me, whether she can trust me or not, to be specific. You've known her a long time, Lottie. Not well, I grant you, but for many years. Try to pry out of her what she would like to do with her life. Find out what she's enthusiastic about. If we know what makes her tick, maybe we can help her jumpstart that little mechanism."

Two days later I had a chance to spend an hour or so with Belle at a 'Welcome Home' party for Dove. Our chat was superficial for sure, but I was impressed with her intellect and her looks and how thoughtful and careful she was in what she said to me. She chose to talk about me rather than about herself. She did that by asking me good questions about photography, especially war photography. Her questions were so penetrating that I suspected she had written them down before meeting me. The next day, I asked Dove if Belle might have done that to impress me.

"I don't think so," Dove replied. "That's just not her style. She is a quick study, but she's not that calculating."

"Do you think she felt a bit overwhelmed, though, last night?" I asked Dove.

"Overwhelmed? "By what?"

"Well, not so long ago she lost her boyfriend. Recently she lost her dad. You are the toast of the town just back from the Front. It would have been the most natural thing in the world for her to want to stay home last night and avoid all the condolences and hoopla, don't you think?"

"No, I don't think so, Lottie. I agree that she's taken some hard knocks lately, but she is a strong person, really. I think she felt she had to show up last night and she did."

Maybe Dove was right. She knew Belle better than I did. But then there was that a fourth factor. Had I made it up, or was it a creation of my own experiences and imagination? It was the Arthur-Dove relationship. It had been so close to perfect, so gratifying to each that it might possibly have left poor Belle feeling inferior to her sister and unloved by her father. Oh well, only time would tell that one. Now we had only to find her a job.

Dove broke into my reverie about Belle's future by asking me about my own difficult early years.

"Lottie, how did you survive the loss of two sisters and your mother as a youngster? We've never talked about this."

"I don't really know how. I do remember some minister telling me to "surrender my worries the Lord," so that's what I did. I reminded God several times a day that I would try to do everything He asked of me each day, but that one day I might just collapse from fatigue or worry or scarlet fever or something else. That was the high-water mark for religion and me, I'm afraid, and it wasn't very high."

"But you gained something from those hardships too, Lottie, don't you think?" Dove suggested. "You probably have some pretty well-founded opinions about what it takes to survive a tragedy like that, don't you?"

"Yeah, I guess I do."

As the party broke up, Dove took me aside and said, "I don't want to find Belle a job. I want to find her something meaningful and gratifying. She deserves it. I'm working on this too. Let me know if you have any ideas."

I told Dove I would see what I could do. Belle spent considerable time at Dove's house. Since I was living there, my access to her was frequent, but she seemed quite guarded when speaking to me. I wouldn't be able to establish any trust or rapport with this smart lady if she thought I was acting pushy or unnatural, so I decided to let her take the initiative and let the friendship grow if it could.

Several mornings later I waltzed into the kitchen and said to Dove, "I've got an idea for you."

"I knew you'd have one, my friend. Talk to me."

"Well, what about offering Belle a job working on our book? She's real smart and could learn to do anything: research, proof reading, correspondence, office bills, etc. You could give her the title of Office Manager. If you get an advance, you'll be able to pay her a real salary and you said yesterday one of the only things she liked in high school was reading good books. Who knows? Just a thought."

"Sounds interesting," Dove said, mulling it over. "She is a smart one. She'd have a lot to learn and a lot to do, but that could be a positive and she's capable of it. Thank you, Lottie. I hadn't thought about this because my relationship with her is a bit shaky. I wouldn't want it to contaminate the whole team. Leg me think about it."

"If you decide to talk to her, don't push her too hard, Dove. I think you may intimidate her somewhat. Easy does it."

When Dove did mention a job to Belle, it was in theory and Belle was flabbergasted. She avoided responding to the offer by asking one question after another. In the end, she made no commitment because it was a theoretical offer.

Dove didn't even have a publisher yet, but she had been working on this requirement. Shortly before the U.S. signed the Armistice Day accord, she was sent to Italy where she met a handsome, young American named Hemingway who was working for the Red Cross as an ambulance driver. One day he received shrapnel wounds in both legs while trying to rescue a wounded soldier. Dove never wrote a word about her feelings for this young man, but it may be that she arranged to stay in Italy for an extra week or two so she could nurse him back to health. In talking about their hopes for their books, Hemingway wrote his name and address on a piece of paper and said, "If you ever get serious about this, let me know. I have some good contacts in New York who might be interested in your ideas.

Though the idea of writing a book about her experiences on the Western Front seemed far-fetched at first, it seemed more doable the more she thought about it. There would be great interest in the subject matter, of course, which would make it attractive financially. And they had almost a year's worth of Lottie' photos to illustrate it. So, under the heading of nothing ventured, nothing gained, Dove dug out Mr. Hemingway's address during her Savannah recovery period and wrote him a note. It was time to take another chance.

A month later, a postcard arrived. It was succinct. "If you don't hear from Snyder and Son, let me know. Hem." His note was followed by an appointment card giving Dove a date and time for a personal interview with the publisher himself, Mr. Robert Dannenberg. She was elated until she noticed she had been given only fifteen minutes for the meeting.

"A twenty-four-hour train ride for a fifteen-minute interview!" she complained.

"How many other publishers are you scheduled to interview?" I asked. Dove shot me a sour look. "Well, get to work, missy. You got to make the most of it. Don't forget you're a woman. Use all your guile."

Sometime after Dove and Belle discussed the idea, Belle spotted a train ticket to New York on the kitchen counter and immediately made the connection. "Hey, Sister, is this what I think it is?" she asked.

"Yep, I have an interview there. It's with a publisher."

"Oh my!" Belle said. "I better get ready."

"What? Does that mean you've decided to work with us?"

"No. You get the publisher first. Then I'll tell you. But you'll convince him, Sister. I'm not worried about that part of the project."

After Belle had left, Dove said to me with a smile, "That was the longest, most civilized conversation we have had since I returned." Dove and I sat in the kitchen most of the morning drinking coffee and discussing the book.

Dove took the train to New York and arrived a day before her interview. She wanted to have a day alone in her room to think about what she wanted to convey and how she wanted to say it. Words were the key. After all, Mr. Dannenberg made his living by judging how effectively people selected their words. Dove worked out some catchy phrases and some plays on words and discovered some issues to avoid. She thought of her father often and wished he were with her. After a good night's sleep, she took a taxi to the publisher's address and arrived an hour early. She and her father's spirit sat in a coffee shop on the ground floor and polished her pitch. She was relaxed and ready as she rode the elevator to their thirty-eighth-floor office.

Having done some research into Mr. Dannenberg, Dove had filled her pitch with words of patriotism, hope and optimism which dovetailed nicely with the prevailing atmosphere in the country. Mr. Dannenberg also sensed a hunger for good books growing across the land. "I can't prove it or explain it yet," he told Dove, "but I can sense it. If we do your book the right way, we'll have a success on our hands."

"Do I understand then that you want to publish my book?" she asked.

"Yes, I do indeed," said the boss. "We'll do the paperwork this afternoon, standard contract for a first book. Hope that meets you're your approval."

"Will I get an advance?"

"Of course, Dove. This afternoon tell us how much you want. We do this by the year."

To everyone's astonishment, the meeting lasted a full

hour. Since Mr. Dannenberg was known to be pathologically punctual, the reasons for Dove's overstay became a major curiosity among the in-crowd at Snyder and Son. Of all the rumors circulating through the offices after Dove's departure, only one made sense: Mr. Dannenberg, who could smell a bestseller a mile away, had been excited by her ideas.

Dove called me as soon as she was sure the deal was closed and to ask what Belle's position was.

"Well, your little sister isn't at home at the moment," I told her. "Do you want me to tell her to make up her mind and let us know right away, or do you want to find out when you get home."

"Let's play it cool now, just for fun. If she comes home and wants to know what's happened, tell her you haven't heard from me yet."

Belle didn't always stay at home if she were visiting from New York. She often stayed with a high school friend, so I didn't worry about her. Dove took the overnight train, which arrived at 9 a.m., and walked through the front door at 9:30.

She poured a cup of coffee, we sat for a few minutes, and she said, "I have something important to tell you. Since you may be working closely with Belle, you need to know that about a year ago she had an ungodly experience. The family doesn't ever talk about this matter, so please don't ever mention it to anyone other than me.

"As you know, for years young Army guys have been making the pilgrimage from Fort Bragg to Savannah to take out our young southern belles. I've heard it said we have a reputation for being fast and easy," Dove said with raised eyebrows. "Well, sometime after she graduated from high school, Belle fell for one of these fellows who was stationed at Fort Bragg. She had been seeing him for about half a year, which wasn't much in real time because the Army Air Corps made it difficult for its paratrooper volunteers to visit Savannah. Back then the paratrooper units were new and highly experimental. They made their first successful jump in March 1912. General Billy Mitchel was their most ardent supporter and wanted their development to remain secret. Therefore, the Army made it difficult for its young paratroopers to fraternize with local civilians. A 24-hour pass was the longest they would issue for a trip to Savannah; a car was essential because the bus was too slow; and its 250-mile distance, one-way, discouraged most young men, but not the captain.

Despite the military's attempts to keep the press away from the Fort, the following article appeared in the Savannah newspaper several weeks after the accident." As she explained the history of the article to me, Dove carefully took an envelope from her purse, removed a yellowing article from it, and handed it to me. I read it aloud:

"On 22 May 1918, Lieutenant John Weinhart of St Luis Obispo, California, died in a parachute accident at Fort Bragg, Georgia. He was making his third jump of the day from 1,200 feet. His first two jumps were routine. Signatures on the primary chute and the back-up belly-pack were Lt. Weinhart's, indicating he had packed both chutes himself. Eyewitnesses said Lt. Weinhart free fell for about 200 feet before pulling his rip cord. This is standard procedure in a 1,200-foot jump. The chute failed to deploy fully. Part became tangled in the risers; the remainder opened into a streamer. When this occurred, Lt. Weinhart went immediately for his belly-pack, back-up chute. Defying all odds, this second chute also failed to deploy properly. It bag-locked, meaning that the pilot chute did not pull the main chute from its box. At about 1,000 feet, with ten seconds to live, several of Lt. Weinhart's buddies saw him take something out of his breast pocket and write on his left hand. He hit the ground, saturated by many recent rainstorms, at about 100 mph. The force of impact drove the entire body between 12 and 18 inches below the surface of the landing zone. The note on the palm of his left hand said, 'luvd u guys' and made the lieutenant an instant legend.

I hate to ask this, but how did Belle find out? Hopefully not from this article?"

"Well, yes, she did learn about it from an Army officer who gave her the semi-official Army death notice. Lt. Weinhart must have been keeping his affair with Belle as quiet as she was because the news didn't travel fast or very far to the best of our knowledge. Arthur and Genevieve took time off from their jobs and devoted all their energy to their wounded daughter. I mentioned to Belle's psychiatrist that Genevieve had lost her boutique as a result of the time she was away, and the psychiatrist replied, "But she saved a daughter." And then he added, "She can always buy another store."

"God, Dove, what a story. The poor thing, at such a vulnerable age too, and a death that is so visually horrid."

"That's what her psychiatrist emphasized. It was so easy to visualize and so difficult not to. I told you this awful story," Dove explained ...

"Before you go further, I'm sure you know that her, or their, accident would have a bearing on my willingness to work side by side on our book project, right? I'd rather be there, keeping a close watch on her ... we don't want any unseen regressions."

"Thank you, Lottie, I can't imagine a better person to be by near her every day than you. You played the same role for me at the Western Front. Oh, I'm so glad that's over. Lottie, like you were with me at the Front." Then, as if to end this tragedy on a positive note, Dove said, "I talked with Belle's doctor yesterday." She hesitated, smiled, and added, "The doc no longer considers her a suicide risk." The two women applauded themselves briefly right there in the kitchen, but Dove, drawing on her years of experience, as a nurse, issued a warning.

"Don't forget, Lottie, young women of Belle's age are particularly vulnerable and fragile, and we don't *know* if she's out of the woods yet." Then, with a slight emotional tremor in her voice she added, "And I for one will always believe that fall almost killed Belle too." A long moment of silence followed Dove's comment.

Dove stood up abruptly and said, "You want a cigarette? I gotta have one, but I threw mine out the other day. I'll be right back," she said as she headed for the cellar stairs to grab a pack from her secret stash. Dove had the wrappings off the pack before she sat back down at the table. We smoked ravenously and in silence for a minute or two.

"You know, the hard part's not quite over yet, Dove," I said breaking the silence as gently as possible. "We have not yet heard Belle's decision about whether she's going to join the team, and I have had a revelation of sorts."

"Oh shit, what now?" Dove barked and I knew I had her undivided attention.

"I had a moment of lucidity this morning," I began. " It was as if a strong wind had blown through my brain and removed all the dust, dirt, and clutter up there and what remained was a single, simple truth. That truth is: the best thing for Belle to do now is to hitch her wagon to her big sister's star for a year or two. Why? Several reasons. First, because it would broaden her knowledge and outlook at a time when she needs both. It would also put her in touch with some of Dove's international contacts. She'd get some exposure to the book business and probably to the nuts and bolts of writing. There is no telling where this might lead. And the most important reason by far for doing this is that you both want it. Belle idolizes you, Dove. She has missed out on your tutelage and your affection. And you, my friend, need to start sharing those things so you can get rid of the bad case of the guilts you have had since we departed France.

"So, sell her on this as soon as you see her. I'll make myself scarce." At that moment the back door opened, and Belle walked in looking worried. "What's the matter, Sister Belle?" Dove asked.

"Nothing, I hope. I'm just a bit nervous about your interview. I thought you were coming home tomorrow. When I saw your car in the driveway, I figured it hadn't gone so well. What's the story? Do we have a contract?" Dove and I looked at each other.

"Your sister should have been a salesman," I said. We watched Belle's face as she processed the words.

"Does that mean you have a deal? That you sold it to them? Oh, my God," she squealed. "Do you mean they offered you a real contract?"

"Yep, to all three of your questions, with a nice advance too. But she has one condition," I added. I waited long enough to allow several possible obstacles to pass through Belle's brain and wipe the smile off her face. It was suddenly so quiet in the kitchen that the light rain falling against the windows sounded loud.

"Okay, what's the condition?" Belle shouted.

"That you be a part of it," Dove answered. "I'd be so happy if you'd be a member of our little team."

"I will," she said evenly.

With that, I walked to her and gave her a hug. Curiously, she made no attempt to hug me back. It made me think she hadn't been hugged in a long time. At the same time, Dove walked behind Belle and gave her a quick shoulder rub and a kiss on the cheek.

"This was a good start," Dove said to me later. "Thanks for the idea."

Although Mr. Dannenberg may well have believed everything he said to Dove that morning in New York, he didn't say everything he believed. For example, he did not say that he did not believe that a thirty-year-old nurse, who had not written anything longer than a prescription, would be able to write a 200-300-page treatise on a world war. He didn't want to tell Dove that he didn't believe she could do that, and he didn't have to because he was the boss. Mr. Dannenberg would hand that delicate duty off to the best man for the job.

That man's carefully chosen name was Ré Rothschild. He was a longtime employee of Snyder and Son and a fountain of academic and intuitive knowledge of literature and authors, and what made each successful. He loved the written word with all his heart and from it he had learned to be a keen, insightful observer of people. On the other hand, his smart-ass, opinionated comments and his thin skin and flamboyant dress made for frequent hard or hurt feelings. He had the pale complexion of a redhead, but his hair was fading to orange with age, and Ré felt the two colors clashed dreadfully. He was involved in consultations with several stylists in New York about how to solve this problem.

After getting his orders from Mr. Dannenberg, Ré called and explained the situation to his old friend Michel Lyon.

"Are you free to take on this project? It has all the ingredients: love, war, death, drama, and man's humanity and inhumanity. Really, it's a writer's dream. This could be your ticket; I kid you not."

Michel, a thirty-three-year-old, French-born, American-educated freelance journalist, was the man both Ré and Mr. Dannenberg had in mind. Michel liked to say he had covered every skirmish and armed conflict that had occurred in the past twenty years, which was a slight exaggeration, but only slight. For a war-hardened journalist, Michel filled his reporting with haunting anecdotes and descriptions of those who suffer most from war. From the Mideast he wrote: "A little boy, one refugee among thousands, up since daybreak, shuffles along a stony road on bloody feet. The blazing sun reflects off a shard of glass on the roadside and draws the boy's attention to a pair of reading glasses. He takes them to his mother. One lens is intact; the other has been cleanly pierced by a small caliber slug. The hole is dead center; blood spatter coats the fake gold frames. The woman screams and drops the glasses. The little boy looks down at them and says, 'Ba Ba?'" The man who wrote those words was not thinking of the men shooting guns, killing, and winning battles," Ré said to an office mate. "No, he was aching for the orphan, for the Mama and Baba, and perhaps for a puppy, whose family threw him into the street because they had no food for him. Who knows?"

Michel believed some men, himself included, were addicted to the life-and-death excitement of war. If they were not addicted, he reasoned, they would never do what they do. He illustrated it as follows: "The imminent threat of a violent death jerks all your senses onto high alert and quiets the noise in your head. From one hundred meters you can see the wind move the feathers along the leading edges of a vulture's wings as it lunges into flight from a tree. Did something spook him? You can distinguish the soft swish-swish of the bird's beating wings from the coarser swish-swish of the enemy's pant legs rubbing as he runs. You hear him clearly, then you don't. You feel his presence as if he were right there in plain view; but he isn't. If he has you in his crosshairs, you could be dead before the sound of his weapon reaches you. If he suspects you have him in your sights, he will move, perhaps too quickly, and squander his advantage."

"I'm free and clear to go, my friend," he replied to Ré's inquiry, "and thank you for thinking of me. When do we start?"

"We leave this afternoon by train," Ré said. "I'll be the trail boss of this project. I'll have to make sure those children don't kill each other, at least until after the book is written, and to make sure it's written by 1 November next year. So, my first priority will be to persuade Dove that she wants you to be the writer-in-chief. If she doesn't go along with that, we're fucked. I'm not worried about it though, so long as you're capable of writing some good copy for about two hours tomorrow morning."

As Ré and Michel discussed their new project, Dove and I were having a quiet lunch. We must have been engrossed in our own thoughts when out of the blue she said, "You know, he was the single most appealing kid I knew in that whole damn war and I miss him every day – especially today for some reason." Her words were choked with emotion. I knew she meant Pete and I knew not to reach across the table and touch her hand. That would have made matters worse. Part of Dove's gospel was 'never compare patients.' She stuck by her rules usually, but that day that rule was no match for Sgt. Pete Rosi's mischievous Sicilian eyes. She said she could hear him saying, "You can't keep me down, Lovey Dovie. You know that, don't you?"

~ ~ ~

Their overnight train from New York arrived at nine in the morning. Ré had agreed to meet Dove at an out-of-the-way coffee shop on Oglethorpe Street at noon. The men checked into their hotel. Ré showered, had a brief nap, changed his clothes, and popped into Michel's room before he left. He was delighted to see Michel sitting behind his portable Remington pecking away.

"Don't fall asleep, Mikie dear. You are the only one who sits between us and failure."

"Out. Get out! Genius at work."

"Give it hell, Mikie. The book will be worth it."

"Yeah, I know it. Go!"

Ré had half an hour to kill before meeting Dove. He

143

walked at a leisurely pace along the river, collecting his thoughts for the day. Having just come from a cold and windy New York, Savannah's Indian summer felt luxurious on his skin. He arrived at Connie's Café relaxed and refreshed, but this would not last. It would be a day of reckoning for all.

As he entered the shop, Ré asked for us and the receptionist led him to a small, private room in the back. Dove greeted him with a handshake. I thought I felt or saw some tension there. They reminded me of two prize fighters touching gloves before round one. There was a great deal at stake for both sides. I thought it interesting that he didn't smile at all when he shook hands with me, nor did he say a word. He just nodded. I was too plain, perhaps, for the man in the purple velvet tie or, more likely, he was preoccupied. I did consider his attire a poor business decision, though. How did he know we weren't hyper-conservative folks who would be offended by such dress? On the other hand, dressing as he did showed me that he was either not at all concerned with the possibility of offending us or he was trying to intimidate us by playing the hard-nosed New Yorker part. I did get the impression that he was intrigued with Dove. He used her name three times in a few minutes and held her chair for her when she sat down. After ordering a hot tea and toast, Ré got down to business.

"Dove, we know you briefed Mr. Dannenberg on your ideas for your book, and he has spoken to me about it, but just to put us all at the same starting place, why don't you tell me briefly what you hope to accomplish with your book."

"Sure," she said. "First, I would like to introduce America to her soldiers. The country would be very proud of them if they were better known. These wonderful boys and young men sacrificed so much for us: their bodies, their families, their dreams and their very lives. I want to write a book about them as an acknowledgement of their contributions and as a thank you. Secondly, I want to show our citizens through words and photos how tragic war is and I must say, Ré, we are grateful to Snyder and Son for your support of this unconventional idea."

"I presume you have never written a book before?" Ré

asked rather awkwardly.

"No, never have. The thought is a little daunting, I admit, but stranger things have happened. Wouldn't you agree?"

Her question tripped him momentarily.

"Well, yes. I suppose they have," he eventually replied. "In any case, it's a magnificent goal, and well put." Then he added, quietly, "Also, I must tell you how much I admire your sense of responsibility to your "boys," those who survived and those who didn't."

He had the tone right, I thought, but his timing was off and he shouldn't even be talking of those who didn't survive anyway.

"I can't imagine any promise we make in life being more sacred than the one we make to a person on his death bed."

Not heartfelt. Too slick. I can't listen objectively. All those young boys. How polite and grateful they were despite their awful wounds. I wish that man would stop smirking.

When I finally looked up at him, he was saying, "And lastly, I must tell you, Dove, that writing the book you envision isn't a job for an amateur. It'll run at least 150 pages depending on page size. It will be filled with complicated relationships between individuals stressed to the limits by war; it will have to deal to some degree with the politics and policies of the warring countries. Forgive my directness but asking you to capture all this in words would be like asking a professional writer to intubate a wounded soldier. If the writer tried to do your job, the soldier would die, and if you tried to write your book, the one you have in mind, the project would die. The nurse and the writer each have highly developed skills, but they are not interchangeable."

I wondered how long he'd worked on that comparison but admitted later to Dove that it was not bad.

"I have a solution to our problem, though. I know a man who is capable of writing this book, although he would need your assistance. His name is Michel Lyon. Michel is French for Michael, but he prefers the French pronunciation to Michael or Mike. He has written two books of his own and has covered every skirmish and every military action that has occurred in the last twenty years, including your war, Dove.

He's a peach of a man; smart, experienced in the heartache of war, and compassionate. When you get to know him, ask him to tell you about the time he saved a little boy who was caught in the middle of a firefight. It's quite a story. Anyway, I'm qualified to say these nice things because I have known him for almost twenty years."

"Michel and I took the train here from New York last night. He worked on his version of our Introduction for some time last night and again from 6 to just before 9 this morning. I went to sleep last night with the click-click, tap-tap of his trusty portable Remington ringing in my ears. I haven't read his version of it yet, but I have it here," he said raising his hand and waving Michel's six pages in the air. He handed it to me just as I entered Connie's Café this morning. "Dove, do you have your copy of our Intro?"

"Right here," she said, placing it in front of him.

Ré drew in a deep breath, and said to Dove, "Now, since this is your story, your book, and your profits, if there are any, *you* have to make the big decisions. If you select Michel as your writer, your first job will be to collaborate with him to produce an outline. Then, as he writes to the outline, you will provide him details and atmospherics to make the text come alive. For example, you might have to describe what you saw, smelled, and heard upon leaving the OR at 4 a.m. after ten hours of surgery. Things like that. What do you think?" Could you do that?"

"Well, you just never know now, do you, Ré?" Dove said coolly. "We'll just have to wait and see if I'm capable of doing my job." Behind the expressionless mask she was wearing, Dove's face was probably red with rage. For over a year she demonstrated she could do a life and death job under the worst of conditions. Now this insensitive, rude little man, who had been living well in New York throughout the war, was questioning her abilities to describe an OR.

As Ré spoke, Dove saw her next year's work appearing before her. She knew that her real job was to ensure that nothing stand in the way of the realization of her dream. The book had to be written. To do this, she was going to act as liaison to Sawyer & Son so as to keep them happy and meet all their bureaucratic requirements on time. If Mr. Dannenberg developed any reservations about his commitment to this project, it would be Dove's responsibility to know about them early and figure how to revive the publisher's belief in it. Dove also announced that she was going to approve every word and photo that went into the book. This meant that she was going to have to read every paragraph carefully and study each picture individually as well as how it fit in with the pictures around it. The consensus was that she had a good ear for how a sentence should sound when it rolls across one's tongue and a good eye for the pictures she discussed with Lottie and Michel. When she insisted that something be changed, at least I understood why. She would also have to keep her own little workforce happy. After all, that was where the work was going to be done. She didn't expect that this would drain much of her energy, but only time would tell. Finally, she would have to provide written descriptions of places, situations, and moments that Michel had not seen or experienced. She was to find that this took up most of her work time. She was going to be a busy girl for the next year, but she was confident they could do it.

As she was finishing some notes she had taken during Ré's remarks, Ré sidled up behind her and said, "The book title will be your decision. Below the title it will say *by Katherine Colombé as told to Michel Lyon*. You will get first billing. Michel is available and probably getting a little anxious, wondering when the jury will finish its deliberations. Would you like to meet him now, or after you have made your decision?"

"Afterward, thank you, Ré. I won't be in the office, but I'll be in touch."

As Dove and I left the café, Dove said to me, "Did he just make a fool of me?"

"No, not at all. You did fine."

After Dove and I had read both versions of the Intro, Dove went outside for a smoke and I called Belle and asked her to come to the office right away. While waiting for Belle, I read Michel's six pages two more times. It was a thing of beauty. When Belle arrived, she sat at her new desk, placed Michel's six pages in front of her, and started to read.

Three minutes later she said, "Holy shit," and began to cry. She read it two more times, daubing her tears as she read. "I can't believe I'm doing this," she said. "I think we have a winner. What do you think?"

Dove and I nodded our agreement. Dove then called Michel and asked him to come to the office, alone.

"The pages you wrote are really stunning, Michel," Dove said. "I was moved almost to tears, but I learned how not to cry in France. In fact, that might be a title. *Learning Not to Cry*. What do you think?"

"Could be," he said, "although we don't want anything that needs interpretation, not in the title. I've been thinking about *17 Million*."

"Oh, I like that," Dove said. "It emphasizes the anti-war theme, which is the purpose of the book, and it's short and memorable. You're not bad at this game, Michel," she teased him.

The four of us talked until cocktail hour, and then right through it. Loosened by the excellent white wine I was drinking, I asked Michel if we reminded him of the French classic, *The Three Musketeers*. Dove, ever alert, raised her glass and said, "And now we are four."

"All for one, and one for all," Michel said, reciting the Musketeers' motto. "*Un pour tous, et tous pour un,*" he repeated in French. Dove must have liked the way the conversation – and the alcohol – was flowing because she discreetly called Connie's Café and ordered six take-out dinners. By the time they closed Connie's, the Four Musketeers were vowing to meet before breakfast in the morning to write a Musketeer theme song. Earlier in the evening, each had taken the measure of their new partners and searched for indications that the group would coalesce. Belle was actively social all evening and, I would guess, was feeling a little high as I walked her to her car. Apparently, she had been keeping her eye on Michel, whom she described as "tough on the outside, soft on the inside."

"How did you come to that conclusion?" I asked.

"By analyzing his writing and his face," she replied.

"Gaiety's inconsistent with all the death and sadness he has seen. So, you have a man who doesn't smile often, but that doesn't mean he is not affected by what he has seen. To write like he does requires great sensitivity, don't you think, Lottie?" I nodded. "And he looked strong and fit and, judging by the rate at which he was bouncing his knee up and down under the table, he probably has more energy than ten eight-year-old boys." A brief silence ensued. "He was telling me yesterday that when he was on and writing well, he could go for twelve hours at a time. Plus, he's pretty good looking for an older man. Good night."

The next morning, I was with Dove when Ré appeared in the lobby of his hotel to meet her. He was visibly angry. She did not acknowledge his mood, but immediately set about telling him that she had chosen Michel as their writer-in-chief and that the team had spent the night getting to know one another. Ré apparently knew this and felt that he had been excluded from last night's activity.

"You are welcome to stay as long as you wish, of course," Dove said, "but to produce this book in a little over a year is going to require long days and short vacations starting today. My suggestion is that you give us two weeks to produce an outline, then come down and see what you think. Now, one last matter. I know we did not get off to the ideal start. As a peace offering, I want you to have this American flag. It flew over one of our hospitals throughout the Battle of the Somme. Let me know when you have your return schedule so I can meet you at the train station. On your future visits, by the way, you are welcome to stay in my house if you wish. Stay in touch and safe travels. I've got to get to work." Dove had not given Ré a chance to speak a single word during their farewell interview. This made me uncomfortable, so I shook his hand and told him I hoped we would have a chance to spend time together on his next visit.

Work began that day. Belle and I had rented a suite which gave us two good sized offices, one for Dove and Michel and one for Belle and me. We envisioned using the two extra rooms for my photos and Belle's research papers and books. Having been office employees for years, Michel and I quickly marked our territories and established our routines, but Belle was going to need more time.

At the beginning, Belle's attitude around her sister was passive and servile. Suspecting that she would be a little nervous, Michel and I asked her questions that were safe and easy to answer. Gradually, Belle and Michel connected and a long discussion of their roles and where and how they differed and how to fulfill them. At least one major decision resulted from their long morning talk: their office would be called 'the engine room.'

As we left the office one night I said to Michel, "Have you had a chance to talk to Belle yet?"

"Yes and no," he answered. "We had some good talks about work, but nothing personal yet. I like her a lot, though, and she picks things up fast. I'm sure we'll be able to work well together."

"Well, that sounds like an excellent beginning," I said. Then cautiously I added, "Wouldn't it be great if we could help her a little while we're working together?"

"Sure would," Michel replied, and that was enough for then. I didn't want to siphon off any of the creative energy he was using to write, and I didn't know him personally very well, so I decided to let things take their own course.

Working with Michel was easy, though. His only request was for quiet. "I can't concentrate if there is music playing or people conversing near me," he announced to his fellow Musketeers during our first week of work. He and I spent time every day that first work week looking for photos that would complement well the narrative he was writing at the time. Occasionally, Dove joined us to kibitz. She had veto power over all photo placements and an excellent eye for this kind of work. She really didn't bother us too much.

Belle especially worked furiously during those first weeks, soaking up knowledge on spelling, punctuation, and grammar and improving her research skills. As her contributions in this area increased, Michel's morale improved because he felt freer to concentrate on his writing and less on spelling and syntax and the like. Belle's spirits improved too as she began to feel she was making a substantive contribution. Michel and I let her work as much and as hard as she wanted to, sensing that it was good therapy, and we awarded her the title editor-in-chief. In the meantime, our leader, Dove, watched over the coalescence of our personalities, preferences, and peculiarities. She asked me occasionally how the Three Musketeers were getting along. "Are you," she asked.

"Yes, we are," I replied. "But you surely are one of us. We are four."

One cold morning around Thanksgiving, as Belle was pulling on her jacket to go for coffee, I said, "One second, I'll go with you. We sipped our coffees at Connie's that morning without saying much until two boys in uniform came in. Their fore and aft caps were decorated with the cloth patch of the paratrooper trainees. Belle eyeballed them for a long minute and said, "I had a boyfriend who was a paratrooper. Did you know that?"

Having vowed never to lie intentionally to Belle, I said, "Yes, but not much." Trying to sound very nonchalant, I added, "What was the deal with him?" That didn't sound good at all. I even thought I saw Belle wince at the question, and said immediately, "I'm sorry I didn't mean to ..."

"No, no that's okay. I should be able to talk about him. He was a bit older than I. He'd come to Savannah unexpectedly, take me out to dinner, tell me how pretty I was, then I wouldn't see him for another month or two. Their training schedule was very hard though, because the paratroopers were an experimental force then. I was always hopeful and frequently disappointed, and I never got used to having to share my love with an Army unit. Jack really loved what he did, and I don't think that he'd ever change in that regard." She paused for a long time but, like any good therapist, I didn't interrupt her contemplation. Finally, she said, "Yeah, the way he treated me, even including the way he died on me, made me angry. I still am, to be honest, but I'm making progress, really. You don't have to worry about me. He was very handsome and fit like all those paratroopers and he was proud of himself for doing what he was doing. It must have been a good time of life for him, except I seldom think of him that way. I always gravitate quickly to his last two minutes of his life ... The sheer horror of it. God, can you imagine?"

"I don't know what to say, Belle. How absolutely awful!" I reached across the table and held her hand. "Do you ever have bad dreams about it?"

"I don't dream much, but when I do, it's always the same dream and it's always about the accident."

"It sounds to me like it's still a part of your subconscious," I replied. "Given your boyfriend's demise and your reaction to it, I wonder if you should spend the next year writing a book that is primarily about death. What do you think?"

"Yes, I know, Lottie, but I like what we've got going now at work. In researching and telling your story, we three have a chance of awakening hundreds, maybe even thousands of people to this monstrously stupid slaughter man engages in routinely in the name of some cause. I almost feel we have a *duty* to finish the book, don't you?"

We continued our discussion until the two paratroopers stood up to leave. As the boys passed Belle's table, she looked up, smiled adoringly and gave them her sexiest version of the 82nd Airborne's motto "All the Way."

On our walk back to the office, Belle said, "I'm going to try to find out what Michel has to say about the mass murdering that went on during the war. The world can't afford to lose seventeen million of its young men very often, right?"

"I don't know about those statistics, but if Michel does, I'd be interested in hearing what he has to say."

When Michel and Belle came back to the office after a brisk autumn walk, they were in a serious discussion and didn't notice that Dove was in her office. Michel was saying, "I'd rather live to be eighty, of course, but if I only live to be only fifty, who's going to know the difference? Not me, that's for sure."

"But you're thinking only about yourself, Michel," she pleaded, using the French pronunciation of his name. You're not taking death seriously because you refuse to think about how your death would hurt others. Think about that little boy you saw when he found his *Baba's* glasses. That death could wreck that little human being's whole life."

"It probably won't though," Michel said as if he didn't

152

have to think much about that child to know how his life would turn out. "Chances are his life will be pretty bleak whether those were his father's specs or someone else's. He'll get over it though. He may even grow up to be a bomb thrower."

"You are such a windbag, Michel," Belle said gently. "You would like to hide your feelings about that little boy and many others, but instead you have written about them. You have granted them anonymity, but you have also given them publicity. I wouldn't be surprised to learn you have all their names and addresses in a safety deposit box and you're hoping to send each of your little kids a check from your book's proceeds. You can hide their names, but the beautiful things you saw in them reveal much more than you can hide."

"You're talking gibberish, woman," he said raising his voice, "but people see things all the time in my writing that I didn't intend. Tell Dove I won't be back this afternoon." On his way out, Michel walked by Dove's office. He saw her there but did not stop to say anything.

Dove came out of her office, looked at Belle and said, "Trouble in paradise?" This was the first time she had acknowledged that Belle might have some feelings for Michel.

"The guy's deceiving himself and that's not healthy," she charged.

"Let me stop you right there. In some cases, self-deception is a form of self-protection. I think Michel may belong in that category."

"How long were you listening?"

"I was here when you and Michel came back from lunch."

The next two days at work were uncharacteristically quiet. On the third day, Belle came in with four coffees and a treat for Michel. On a lark, she had asked an old friend who was the owner of Savannah Pastries if he could make a giant glazed donut, Michel's favorite food. He could, and did, and as Belle handed Michel his donut, she said, "Michel, I'm deeply sorry I pushed you so hard the other day. I had no reason to criticize your writing – I think you're a genius at what you do – nor did I have any right to tell you what you were thinking. If you forgive me, I promise never to criticize your work again –

unless you ask me to."

"Let me taste this donut before I give you my answer," he said, taking his first bite.

Belle's conciliatory gesture and the eagerness with which Michel accepted it restored the cooperative atmosphere to their office and powered up the writing mechanism, much to my relief.

The team looked out on rain and grey and brown colors as it started its final push to the end. For Michel, writing the last chapter was always the most difficult. It required tying off all the loose ends and explaining one last time, without blatantly repeating himself, why the knottiest problems persist. Ré knew his friend dreaded "putting a book to bed," so he phoned Michel several times a week to offer him solace and encouragement. He also urged him to keep the book's focus on the fight each soldier faced as he was admitted to one of Dove's hospitals. "Death was relentless," Dove reminded Michel, "but life was every soldier's most precious possession. Life vs. Death. There it is boiled down to its simplest form." One morning, Dove stuck her head in Michel's office and said, "Give it all you got."

Despite Dove's cheerleading, the argument was not settled yet. Belle, the only deferential teammate a year ago when we started, raised her hand, not to ask permission to speak, but to notify her friends that she was going to speak. She stood in order to take control of the conversation.

"I feel strongly that we should lighten up somewhat in the last chapter to give voice to the readers' hopes that this war will, indeed, be the war to end all wars. I bet everybody, victors and vanquished alike, harbor such hopes. In fact, it would be inconceivable if they didn't. And there's another reason, more practical than the first, perhaps, why we should lighten up. We have dealt thoroughly with the nasty subject of death throughout the book, even though one can't learn anything from it because it's an entirely random occurrence. Young people die and old people die. Sick people die, except some don't. My boyfriend died when his parachute failed to open while some other guy fell out of a plane without any chute, went through a barn roof, and landed in a hay loft no worse

154

for wear. If we leave our readers mired in thoughts of the morbid, sad, and depressing subject of death as they finish the book, we will jeopardize our chances of having a bestseller on our hands and make a flop likely. Dannenberg will not be calling us to discuss a follow-up book, and we won't earn much for our labor over the past year. Hope is an American characteristic and I hope we will end our work on a hopeful note."

No one said a word. All eyes were focused on the floor or on the ceiling. After a long pause, Belle said with a broad grin, "I thought so: you guys are afraid of me!"

Michel laughed. "We've been wondering how long it would take you to figure that out." Laughter broke the tension and then Michel continued his defense. "The death of 17 million men has been the focus of our book since the beginning. How can our last scene be of a little girl and her puppy skipping through a strawberry patch, for God's sake?"

I rose in defense of Belle. "You have asked a key question, Michel. I'll answer you in two words: human beings. They can let hope dwindle down to fumes in the worst of times, but human beings never lose hope completely. You don't have to look any further than this room to see that I'm right. Belle lost her first love tragically but hope replaced despair and now she is happy again. In one year when I was a little girl, I lost two sisters and my mother attempted suicide. I was confused and frightened, but I prayed for God to take care of me until my mother felt better. Having God on my side certainly gave me hope. Lastly, I call your attention to Dove and you, Michel. You two have witnessed so much death and destruction. You have seen the worst of the worst and yet just last night I saw you two laughing so hard I thought you were going to pop. I am with Belle. We've got to leave the characters in our book with reason to hope so they can pass their hope along to our readers."

Everyone looked at Dove. It was decision-making time. "Michel," she began, "I don't think either Belle or Lottie were suggesting that you paint a picture of a little girl in a strawberry patch to represent the way we view the state of the world today. In fact, between your vividly descriptive words and Lottie's intimate photos, our readers should come pretty close to being sickened by the look of war close-up. We have accomplished that goal. Thank you. But, just to make it official, I do agree with Belle and Lottie that we should write the last chapter in such a way that both the characters in the book and those real live men and women who will read it will feel some justification for hope and optimism when they close the book and put it on the shelf where they keep the books they intend to read again."

Dove and Michel had already blocked out the last chapter and Dove had approved the photos to accompany it. The baton had been handed to Michel to run the last lap and cross the finish line. The last event of the evening was a brief after dinner speech in which Ré announced that Dove would be leaving soon for a one-month tour of the U.S. to promote her book. His announcement was greeted by boos and catcalls and whistles. Ré was shocked and puzzled. He yelled from where he stood at the head of the table, "What's wrong? What the hell did I say?" Belle's soprano voice soared above the others in response: *un pour tous, tous pour un.* And finally, the chorus inserted itself delicately: one for all, all for one. Still full of adrenalin and team spirit from working so hard to finish the book on time, the Musketeers were insisting that either the four of us would go on the book tour, or, none of us would. We were so overbearing about it that Ré agreed. It was an expensive concession, though, and I never learned who actually footed that bill.

Mr. Dannenberg, anxious to see his predictions for Dove's book come true, threw all of Snyder and Son's resources and know-how at promoting their creation. The book hit the market on 1 December 1920, specifically timed to entice Christmas shoppers. By early March it was on most of the bestseller lists, where it stayed for eighteen months.

FRANCE

The Musketeers did not love being on the road for an entire month, but Michel did. During the first year the book was on sale, Michel traveled extensively promoting it. Dove was particularly grateful to him for emphasizing the book's appeal for peace, as this was really its main purpose. As he said once, "I'm campaigning to put myself out of business as a war correspondent, but sadly I'll never succeed." New York was still his home and headquarters, but when he wasn't there or on the road, he was down in Savannah with "his women," as he called us. He and Dove had built an effective working relationship while writing the book, and afterward watched it transform itself into a friendship that would last the rest of their lives.

But it was Michel and Belle who fell in love. It was an unconventional affair to be sure, one that withstood Michel's always being on call and occasionally having to leave on a moment's notice to record the beginnings of a new war in some far-off land. Over time, Belle became more concerned about the chances of his being hurt or killed but she didn't feel she had the right to ask him to stop. Michel knew of her concerns and continued to pursue his profession, although with considerably more caution than he had exhibited when he was younger. Belle couldn't stew about him all the time he was gone because she had developed her own career as an editor, shepherding several popular books through the obstacles of publication and earning the respect of her colleagues.

On her own and seemingly without promoting herself, Dove had morphed into an American original. Hollywood made a movie out of her book, which led to the writing of two more books, for which she assembled us, the aging Musketeers. The press asked for her opinions and both political parties vied for her support as the world became aware it was on course for another war. Although Dove was only in her early fifties and could have had her choice of several influential jobs, she could not find the commitment she knew she would need to endure another war.

Dove went to see Dr. Alexander Bregman, her friend and classmate from high school. "I'm just not feeling well, Alexander. I don't have much energy; I can feel my heat beat sometimes and I don't sleep very well."

"Why do you think you have developed these symptoms, Dove?

"I have my opinion, Alexander, but I want yours. Why do *you* think I have them?"

"Because you are worried about world events. Having recently lived through many atrocities of war, it must seem like absolute and abject stupidity to see your country preparing to do the same again and yes, I can give you something for your high blood pressure and palpitations, but I'd like you to put your mind to work to solve the insomnia problem."

Dove saw her friend Alexander throughout World War II. Her symptoms did not abate until the war ended and even then her palpitations recurred when she was stressed and she almost never slept soundly. Generally, though, she felt strong enough to go for a two mile walk each morning and to keep up with her invitations and social engagements. As mid-century approached, the French government awarded her the prestigious Inter-Allied Victory medal for her service during World War I. John J. Pershing, the former commander of American forces in Europe, pinned the medal on her at a ceremony in Paris.

I had my birthday while we were in Paris. I was approaching my sixties and thinking about stopping to smell the roses occasionally. My health was good, but I didn't have the stamina I used to have. My reputation as a revolutionary photographer was still intact from our first book, so every month I received two or three inquiries or offers of work. I turned most of them down, but if the location were new to me or particularly inviting, I accepted. Dove still had many interests, obligations, and opportunities that needed someone to look after them. I was that someone, and happy to do it.

I was in the kitchen one evening doing the dishes when I heard Belle say to Dove, "What would you think if I told you ... uh ..."

"That you and Michel were going to be married?"

"Uh, yeah. How did you know?"

"Well, I'd be devastated," Dove replied, with a straight face. "I love him far more than you do."

I heard Belle give Dove a kiss and say. "Thanks, Sister, but that was the easy question."

"Uh oh, what now?"

"We wondered if you would mind if we got married without your being there ... with us ... when we get married, I mean."

"Baby Doll, that just *ain't gonna* happen as long as I'm alive and kicking," Dove replied. "I was just thinking that you could have the wedding right here at the house ..."

"But that's just it, Dove, we want to get married in the same church where Michel's parents were married."

"Oh, I see," Dove said. And she did see. Suddenly she realized the questions were about her, her health, and the wisdom of her traveling to France. Belle apparently thought that the trip might be too much for her even though, when Belle and I had asked Doctor Bregman two weeks earlier about taking her to France, he gave it his full blessings. "Sure, take her with you. It would be fun for all four of you." While his recommendation was reassuring, Belle and I still were not convinced this was a good idea.

Although nothing was decided that night, the delicate issue of Dove's travel, and indeed her independence, had been tabled for family discussion without a punch being thrown.

The festivities were not yet over, however. After saying her thank you and goodbye to everyone, Belle pulled on her coat and headed for the front door. As she was reaching for the doorknob, Dove yelled at her from the other end of the room, "Please think about what you're going to do with that mother of yours and let me know."

"She's your mother too," Belle fired back.

"Well, you got the only telegram anyone in this family has received from her since she left for France. That makes you responsible for replying to her and finding out what the hell she meant in her telegram when she said she had run into trouble with French bureaucrats who were obstructing her efforts to bring her parents to the U.S. She was slightly out of breath. She stopped momentarily then continued. "If I ever see the woman again," she said in an icy tone, "she better have a good reason for not attending her husband's funeral."

Belle drew breath to answer her sister, stared at her for a second or two, and marched out the front door. It was a wise decision. Dove may have been the oldest and the most infirm in her clan, but she was still the matriarch and missing her father's funeral was an offense Dove was unlikely to pardon.

Belle must have taken some deep breaths of Savannah's sweet night, put the family's priorities in proper order, and reentered the house. She was once again going to take the lead in an important family matter. "Okay, ladies, we owe it to Papa to do our best to support Genevieve fully in her hour of need. She did as much for me and more recently she rode off into a dangerous, fluid situation to rescue her own ancient parents. It is possible she feels guilty as hell for missing Papa's funeral, but we know that is what Papa would have wanted her to do. Dove, please get one of your adoring French contacts to pull a string of two and release Genevieve's folks to their daughter's care. Once you do that, I will go and get them if you wish. Just tell me what you want me to do, and I will comply. *D'accord?* But let's get on this tomorrow. I love you both."

As soon as Belle had closed the door, Dove said to me, "So, what do you think, Wise One?"

"I think she's worried about your health and the possibility it could fail while we're traveling in some faraway land. To be honest, I'm concerned about that too. As for travel, I'm going if you go; I'm staying, if you stay. And, in the morning, I'll give you my opinion on whether you and I should go to France for the wedding or not, but now I've *gotta* turn in."

"O come, my dear. Have one scotch with me to celebrate all that lies ahead of us, please. I kicked off my shoes and looked around her handsome living room while Dove poured us a dram each of Laphroaig scotch over three ice cubes, her usual calibration. For a moment it felt like we were about to have a strategy session, but this was not to be a time for calculating. Her feelings took over immediately. She said Belle and Michel's plan to declare their love for each other, in a church no less, had thrilled her and made her happier than she could ever remember. She finished her scotch, poured another, and thought back over the years. She recalled the Four Musketeers' first meeting. It had gone rather deep into the night and by the end of it Belle already had feelings for Michel. She told me that she had often wanted to ask Belle if she thought she and Michel might marry someday, but she had vowed never to intrude in Belle's private affairs and was glad she had had the discipline and wisdom to stick to her vow.

"They seem to have done well for themselves, don't you think?" Dove asked, sipping her scotch and hoping for a little reassurance from me. When I gave it to her, she said, "I'm sure they are in love. It's best then that they decide what's best for them and if some of their decisions affect the old lady, so much the better." She was beginning to slur her words. In all the years I had known her, I had never seen her drunk. "That would just prove they love me as well. I will just abide by their wishes and make some influential calls tomorrow. I'll have all three of them here within a week after the wedding. I'm still good for something."

"Time for bed, Dove." I tucked her forearm in mine and walked her down the hallway to her room. I could tell she was looking forward to tomorrow's activities.

I also must have been wrestling subconsciously with the idea of Belle's marriage. I dreamed she was far from home surrounded by pigs and chickens and people who looked prehistoric. The dream awakened me an hour after I went to bed and didn't allow me to sleep for the rest of the night. By morning light, I had considered all angles of the family situation and all our options and was ready to make my case. I scurried down to the kitchen and there was Dove enjoying her first cup of coffee, playing solitaire, and watching the birds hop around the backyard. I said, "Good morning," and before she could respond, I said, "I think we should all go to the wedding. What the heck! France is not a third world country; they have good doctors there too if we need one. We've got the money. She's your only sister and we ought to be there with her, don't you think?"

Without hesitation Dove agreed. "Good thinking, Lottie. It was one of those things that was so obvious we couldn't see it, but you did. Good for you." And so it was settled, almost. Belle felt she should get Michel's approval before we officially called it 'settled.' Five minutes after that he heard the plan, it was approved unanimously.

We swung into action the next day. Dove made two calls and was assured that her grandparents would be issued unrestricted passports which would allow them to travel as they wished in France. Dove gave herself the responsibility of producing an itinerary which would guide us around the area for about a week and would take us to various landmarks and battlefields that held some personal interest for her. I gave myself the job of sticking close to Dove. She was closing in on a life's goal, which would be filled with nostalgia and emotion. As the realization of this dream drew nearer, Dove became more excited. Her appetite dropped off and so did her sleep. I tried to convince her to conserve her energy so she would have plenty when the show started, but that wasn't an easy task for her or for me.

Belle took responsibility for organizing her own wedding but found that trying to make arrangements by long distance phone in French was fraught with problems. So, she and Michel used their time to plan their wedding in greater detail than they had at home. Whenever Belle became anxious because she wasn't accomplishing anything, Michel would calm her by telling her that within the confines of his home village, Jumiegues, and among its thirty-one residents, he was considered a world-famous man.

"They will do for me, anything I ask," he told her. "So, there is no need to worry, okay?

"Okay, I won't worry because you are world famous." We worked right up to our departure date and found our chores still not completed. We did get to the boat on time and on 1 June 1950 we sailed out of the New York harbor. Our trans-Atlantic journey offered us perfect sunny days and ample ways to pass them, including bridge tournaments, shuffleboard, movies, an old-fashioned ice cream parlor and all kinds of self-improvement lessons. We debarked at Le Havre tanned and rested and checked into a small hotel right at the harbor. Michel admitted he had been unable to rent a car in France while we were in the U.S. He was told repeatedly *"pas de problem, monsieur,"* but he was skeptical. He left the hotel at 8 a.m. and returned at 9:30 with a four-door red Saga. It looked dependable, if not sexy. Michel and I packed carefully – in order to get all the women's clothing in – and we set out to hunt down Dove's ghosts.

Dove had long imagined The Hindenburg Line, but it never seen it. It was a German defensive position built in the winter of 1916–1917, which extended southeast from Dunkirk on the North Sea to the French-Swiss border. The German defenders repulsed every Allied effort to penetrate the line from the spring of 1917 through late summer 1918, dates that coincided precisely with the time Dove and I spent on the Western Front.

Dove had known some of the nurses who were responsible for opening these hospitals and Casualty Clearing Stations as close as possible to on-going battles, but also with good access to rail hubs. A final requirement, preferable but not mandatory, was that they be situated beyond enemy artillery range.

As the family drove southwest generally following the Hindenburg Line, Dove gave Belle, Michel, and me fairly detailed summaries of what had taken place in those storied places. She had memorized the names of the battles, their dates, strategic significance, and casualty statistics. We were impressed.

"Where did you learn all this Dove?" Michel asked.

"I hauled out of the attic in my house all the scrapbooks Lottie's father made for us while we were on the Front.

"Do you still have your scrapbooks, Lottie?"

"Yes, indeed," I replied.

We drove though Arras where the British and the Germans together lost 285,000 men. As we drove between battlefields, Dove recalled for us what life was like in the hospital. "I arrived 6 April 1917, three days after my hospital was overrun for the first time," she explained, "not by

Germans, but by wounded British troops mostly. Our hospital had one hundred beds. The morning I arrived we had 235 patients.

"The name of the small city we will drive through next has become synonymous with war. The total number of casualties in the Battle of Verdun," she said in a solemn voice, "was about 714,000." Dove spoke her statistics in a quiet, expressionless voice, and she was gradually dispensing with the historical commentary. It was the numbers, the hundreds of thousands of killed and wounded and maimed that were on her mind. "It was an unholy slaughter on both sides," she said to no one in particular. The travelers stopped in Verdun for a coffee and to feel the agony and sorrow that pervades the city. We were quiet for a long time after leaving Verdun.

"Don't forget to say a prayer for Pete Rosi," I reminded Dove.

"Already done," Dove replied.

Ten minutes later Dove announced, "And now, *la pièce de résistance,* the hideous and obscene Battle of Somme," she said, spitting out the name. "A million combatants were killed or wounded from July through December 1917. And you know what? After a million deaths, the fighting stopped and both governments declared the battle a draw."

We drove out of town horrified. After passing under several miles of arched canopies of plane tree branches, Belle turned around to say something to her sister and saw one lone tear running down her face. Dove shook her head almost imperceptibly and Belle understood. She turned back to resume looking out the front window, but all she could see was the anguish on her sister's face.

That night we stayed in a country inn that offered both dinner and breakfast. The food was not elegant, but it was fresh: bread still warm from the oven, butter from the barn, ripe tomatoes from the garden, and coq au vin from the barnyard. For breakfast: fresh eggs, croissant from the bakery, and café.

That evening over dinner Dove suggested that we try to find one or two of the buildings that she had converted to hospitals. "It might be fun to go into couple of those buildings," she said. "Don't you think?"

"Do you really think that would be fun for you, Dove? I'm not so sure it would be."

"Oh, Lottie. Sometimes you treat me like I'm an old invalid. Don't you think I'm strong enough to meet those memories?"

"I think you are strong enough, *sans doute*, but you suggested it would be fun. I don't think it would be fun for you to visit places that could stir up those feelings of desperation, sadness, and anxiety that we faced back then. I don't want anyone to hurt you, Dove, including yourself, that's all."

"I know you're just looking out for me, my dear, but I've come all this way and I'm not about to stop now, but thanks," she said, taking my arm to walk down the corridor to her room.

We set out the next morning after breakfast. Dove found a school building she had appropriated – without authority – to use as a hospital. She did this during the height of The Third Battle of Ypres, a struggle that killed and wounded 487,000 men. Fewer men were killed during the first two Battles of Ypres, but the incompetent tactical decision-makers were responsible for hundreds of thousands of unnecessary deaths. Sometime in the early sixties, the school building was restored to its original purpose, education, and a new faculty was assigned to the building. When Michel told the headmaster of Dove's history on the Western Front, he welcomed her as if she were royalty. He called an all-students meeting in the auditorium and begged Dove to tell the students her story, or their school's story. Speaking good French, but with Michel by her side as an emergency interpreter, she summarized her part of the building's long history. Afterward, she held a question and answer period that lasted thirty minutes. The headmaster would not let her go without giving us food. After trying every conceivable excuse, Dove accepted the offer of an omelet. A crisp Chablis and a baguette appeared so the host and honored guest could toast one another. As we drove off, many of the children waved from the schoolyard while Dove smiled coyly at me instead of saying I told you so.

After finding our *pension,* we had a light supper and I

walked Dove to her room. She invited me in for a sherry as she was a night owl and was not ready to go to bed. "Seeing those young, happy faces today was good for me, Lottie. Even though it was many years ago, living with death for a year and a half, as we did, left me with the smell of it always in my nose and thoughts of it unwilling to leave my mind."

I sat next to her and held her hand and nodded from time to time as she spoke. She had something to tell me, so I listened.

"You know, Death can visit you on the spur of the moment, any time, any place, anywhere. The war taught me that. Death just happens. It doesn't ask for our consent or offer explanations. It has no favorites and doesn't seem to know any more than we do about what its next victim will be doing when he feels that cold tap-tap on his shoulder and, poof, he's gone."

We had a long drive ahead of us to Michel's family's village of Jumiegues and then the week of one thousand chores to be ready for the wedding the following Saturday. Nonetheless, we did not leave until early afternoon because we slept late. Belle and I went to the market to buy some fresh bread, some cheese, and a bottle of wine for a picnic along the way. Finally, all was ready. Michel was driving, Belle was next to him, and Dove and I were in the back with her legs stretched out across mine.

"How are you, Sister?" Belle asked. "You seem quiet today. Do you feel okay?"

"I'd love a glass of water," she replied.

Belle smiled at the artful dodge to her question, but she did not push her sister for a direct answer. As an old-fashioned nurse, Dove saw herself as a care giver, not a care receiver. She did pour herself a glass of cool water, though, from our thermos.

In mid-afternoon, we refueled and found a peaceful spot in the countryside overlooking the Seine River. When Michel opened the backdoor, I climbed out and Dove said, "Pull off a piece of that excellent looking bread and let me have another glass of water, Michel, *s'il vous plaît*. I don't want to sit on the ground. It's too hard for me to get up." Belle and I were already meandering ahead looking for a good place to sit and eat.

"That makes sense. Do you want company? We can all eat here with you," Michel said.

"Go on with you," Dove said. As Michel turned to follow Belle and me toward the river, Dove said, "I love you, brother-in-law. I hope you know that."

"*J t'aime aussi*," Michel replied. Hmm. Michel did not mention this exchange to anyone as they ate their bread and cheese, but he thought about it often. When he realized his thoughts had turned from curiosity to concern, he excused himself and walked back to the car as casually as he could. There was Dove, looking entirely at peace and in precisely the same position she was in when he last saw her. He checked for a pulse to be sure: she was not asleep. Michel, the man who had seen everything, dropped to his knees and asked God to take her in.

He gently and tearfully broke the news to Belle and me. He said, "She showed us every day how to live with grace. Today, she demonstrated how to die gracefully."

We put the top up and drove to the village pharmacy from where Michel called the American Consulate in Paris. He spoke to a Vice Consul, Dave Smith, who sounded sympathetic and competent.

"Drive directly to the Consulate, M. Lyon," Mr. Smith said. "Our address is 2 avenue Gabriel. I'll stay here until you arrive. I will notify the Marine guard that I'm expecting you. You concentrate on driving though. It's especially dangerous now because you're upset, and your mind may wander. Do you hear me?"

"Oui," Michel said.

"How far away are you?"

"Less than one hour."

"See you soon."

Michel passed Mr. Smith's instructions along to Belle. "All that is fine and dandy, Michel, but I can't ride for an hour with poor Dove staring at the back of my head."

Michel could feel his senses respond as they had for years in demanding situations around the world. Do whatever it takes, he thought, pulling to the side of the country road.

"I know you can't, *ma Chérie*. I'll take care of it. I promise."

Michel spread out a beautiful Tunisian blanket on a grassy knoll behind the car. They had bought the blanket as a wedding present.

"Ah, you never know," he said out loud.

Although it was not easy or pleasant, he managed to carry Dove from the car, lie her on the blanket, and roll her in it. To make sure she was secure, he synched the top of the roll with one of his belts and the bottom with another. Fortunately, Michel had chosen a car with an external trunk mounting rack and a very large travel trunk. First, he removed the women's clothes from the trunk. Then he took a deep breath and climbed into the trunk. He fit. Therefore, he figured, Dove would fit in it too, as long as she was seated, and her legs were bent. The next step would be the most difficult. He lifted Dove from the knoll, carried her to the car, and with great difficulty he maneuvered her into a sitting position in the trunk. This job took all the self-discipline and strength he could muster. Once finished, he examined the trunk carefully to make sure it was belted securely to the rack. With his last belt, he secured the lid, then he fell into the driver's seat, out of breath, perspiring profusely, and feeling sick to his stomach.

"I am absolutely ashamed of myself for asking you to do that," Belle said. "I'm so sorry."

"It had to be done," Michel whispered, as he turned the key in the ignition with a shaky hand.

"Everybody okay? Can we leave?" Neither Belle nor I said anything. Michel engaged the transmission and the car moved forward. Silence fell over us as we turned for Paris. Each of us was alone, swimming in a flood of emotions: the loneliness and finality of death, the stimulation of adrenalin, and the forever loss of a dear friend.

At 7:45 in the evening, we pulled into one of the many empty parking places in front of the Consulate. We made our way two steps at a time up a long flight of cement stairs to the locked front doors. A guard unlocked the doors and was offering us chairs when Mr. Smith arrived. He calmly introduced himself, expressed his condolences, and asked for Michel's and Belle's passports.

"When I heard you were here, I called the funeral home again," he said. "They promised they would be here within fifteen minutes. So, Mlle. Colombé, would you like to wait in my office while I go with M. Lyon to move your car?"

"No," Belle said. "I'd rather stay with my sister until the man from the funeral home arrives."

"As you wish. And Mlle. Lottie, are you agreeable to a short walk?"

"I am," Lottie said formally.

"Let's go move the car then," Mr. Smith said, beckoning them in the direction from which they had come. "I don't like to leave my car on the street for too long at this time of day." He unlocked the big front door and said, "I'll lead the way. Please watch your step."

Michel and Belle descended the stairs in front of Lottie. Suddenly, the three stopped abruptly on the steps. The car was gone. So was Dove.

Within minutes of his hearing that the car and body had disappeared, the Minister of Interior, Pierre Zieleman, ordered a nation-wide dragnet and promised Belle, Michel and me that he would capture the culprits.

Two weeks later, M. Zieleman suggested we consider going home. "I will keep you informed of any and all significant developments, I promise," he said. "It just seems better for you to have the comfortables of home while you wait rather than sit in these ugly police station, don't you agree?"

Then he turned the tables on us again and said, "I think this is going to be a slow-moving case. Generally, if we don't pick up some worthwhile leads in the first two weeks or so, the prospects aren't looking so good." After mulling over his advice, we found that we agreed with the minister. He hosted a farewell luncheon for us in a lovely French restaurant he claimed was his favorite and two days later we were headed home to Savannah.

For several months after Dove's body disappeared, every policeman and intelligence officer in France had as his first priority the finding of Mme. Colombé. All confidential sources who had given the police any information on auto theft in the past decade were contacted and tasked to find out everything they could about the infamous Colombé car theft. The case was also scrutinized unofficially by every tinker, tailor, soldier and spy in the country, and by every man on the street as well. Curiously, despite the manpower involved and professional and persistent efforts of the police, no clues were found, no scents were picked up.

The total absence in the underworld of rumors or even funny stories about the heist of a car from the U.S. Embassy with a famous cadaver in its trunk struck Minister Zieleman as strange. "The incident is too unusual and darkly humorous to be ignored," he said to several of his senior officers one morning.

"It could be because they are first time carjackers, Sir," a young woman suggested. "That would account for their not making contact with any of our tried and true fencers of hot cars. They probably just didn't know who to call."

"*C'est ça, Mademoiselle,*" the minister said. "You got it! That explains their actions up to this moment. But that dragnet's got to snag them now." But there the Minister ran out of words and his hope seemed uncertain suddenly. The intuition of this old cop told him to say no more, for it was not to be.

Neither the car nor the corpse was seen again. When the French people thought of their friend and admirer being dumped in a hole in a lonely back acre of a farm somewhere, it touched their souls deeply. Services were held spontaneously for her across the country. It was during that month of services that the metamorphosis of Dove Colombé from human being to legendary war heroine began. She would have been amused.

BOTTOMS UP

I had just passed my first college-level final exams and flown home to the handshakes and hugs of my parents and friends. On the way home, my Dad turned off the toll road one exit early so we could drive through the center of our little town and see it decked out in its Christmas lights and traditions. A forty-foot Balsam fir from British Columbia stood in the town square. Front doors and store fronts were trimmed with ingenious arrangements of straw, eggs, berries, flowers, shells, apples, and evergreen boughs, just as they were in 1749 when the town was founded. It was eight o'clock in the evening and the town was bustling. Holiday spirit was in the air.

The next morning, after a Rip van Winkle-like sleep, a bracing shower, and a chocolate croissant still warn from the oven, I walked the two blocks to Grace O'Neil's house with a bounce in my step. She must have seen me from the kitchen window because she was standing on the porch waiting for me as I swung open the gate to their yard. "Hi, G," I said. "How are you?"

Her answer: open arms, big smile, a warm hug and a kiss on the cheek. It was nice to be home.

"Ah, here we are again. Back where it all started," I said.

"Yep. Sitting around the old breakfast table," Gracie said. Before she went to work, Mrs. O'Neil had made coffee and put some pastries in the oven for us.

Grace poured and served, and I jumped started the conversation.

"I brought you a Christmas present," I said, handing her a book-sized package wrapped in Christmas paper.

"Oh, thanks, Henry," she said absentmindedly. She closed her eyes and focused on the package. She was preserving the suspense by unwrapping the package slowly, carefully pulling off each piece of scotch tape and folding the paper carefully so it could be used for a second wrapping. This was one of her little ways. Finally, she held the unwrapped book in both hands. Her eyes were still closed.

"I think it's an old book," she said. "I can tell by the musty smell and the softness of the covers and because there is no book jacket." She felt the inside surfaces of both covers. "No pockets for library cards. Therefore, owned by a private person, a collector let's say. Did you get this at an estate sale, Henry? I know how you love them."

"I bet I know what it is. We read Out of Africa together last summer. Remember? And loved it. I bet it's a signed copy of that book. Is it?" she said opening her eyes.

"Look at the title page," I suggested. She turned the page gently and there under the title Out of Africa in faded blue ink, but still entirely legible, was Isak Dinesen's signature.

"Oh, Henry, thank you so, so much! Imagine, her hand was right here when she signed it. I will treasure it forever."

I knew she really meant it. During the summer before her senior year in high school Gracie visited Tanzania and Kenya with her father, who taught courses in Agriculture at a local university. During that trip, Africa bit Gracie, as the old Africa hands say. She fell in love with it fast and completely, just as Ms. Dinesen had done.

"Would you get some cream out of the fridge, please?"

"Wow looks like a party. Am I invited?"

"Yes, of course. Isn't my Dad thoughtful?"

Yeah, he sure is."

"And speaking of beer," she said seductively, "I have a little Christmas present for you, sailor." With that, she stopped speaking and began lifting her purse by its strap off the back of her chair. She was moving slowly and looking longingly into my eyes over one shoulder. She licked her lips, did the shimmy-shake, and slipped a manila envelope from her purse. Next thing I knew she was sliding individual pieces from the envelope across the table to me and I was holding my first fake driver's license and some authentic looking pocket litter.

"You've got to be kidding me," I managed to say.

"Come on with me, sailor?" she said in a husky voice. "I'll show you my favorite little out-of-the-way bar, or maybe I'll show you something even more interesting. Whaddaya say?"

"You've got to be kidding me," I said again.

"Do you think it's a bad idea?" Gracie asked with a hint of angst in her voice. But her self-confidence quickly returned, allowing her to take a swipe at my new classmates.

"It may be that your exposure to those rich preppies you live with in New England have caused you to lose your nerve or to no longer find this type of undertaking amusing. But I shouldn't prejudge you. Do you want to go, or not?"

I said nothing as I watched the grin spread across her face, a grin that didn't convey humor so much as a taunt or a dare. I had seen it before and was sure she was about to challenge me.

"A bad idea?" I repeated. "We're not talking about ringing doorbells on Halloween anymore, G, or letting the air out of someone's tires. It's against the law to drink in public if you're not at least eighteen and it's illegal for a bar to serve anyone under eighteen. You and I could go to jail and be fined for doing that. The bar owner could lose his liquor license, which would mean losing his business. If that happened, the folks who work for him would lose their incomes, which would be awful for them especially during the holiday season. So, does that sound like a good idea to you?"

"Come on, Henry, don't be such a stick. You know the chances of our going to jail and a bar owner losing his bar, and all of his employees ending up penniless and freezing to death because their only place to sleep was in a snowbank. You know the chances of that happening are so small we don't have to worry about it."

The legal drinking age in our state then was eighteen. Grace and I, unlike most of our classmates, were still seventeen that Christmas. It seemed to us as if our magic numbers – 20 days for me and 29 for her – were somehow resisting the inevitable advance of time. I took this in stride, figuring beer would always be available one way or another, but Gracie was not so passive. Her Latina-Irish genetic make-up was going to explode if she didn't do something. So, she did.

"Now we can go out and drink beer with our friends if we

want to risk getting in trouble with the law, the college and our parents, or we can sit in the kitchen safe and sound with my grandmother. It's up to you," she said.

But there was another issue we had to consider. The sheriff's department had been flooding the airwaves and local papers with threats of jail time and serious fines for violators of the laws on underage driving and driving while intoxicated. It was of concern to us underagers because we didn't know how to evaluate the threat. None of us and none of our parents could recall any such campaign in past years.

I shook my head and realized immediately I had sent the wrong signal. A shake was negative. I didn't mean that ... exactly."

"Do you remember that book you loved? The author was a mountain climber who intentionally put himself and real danger once in a while to see if he could still think well and respond physically under life-threatening pressure

"Yes, of course I remember it, but ..."

"Well, maybe you've changed," she suggested. "Maybe you need to test your reflexes like your friend the rock climber to see if you've still got what it takes." She looked at me intently for several seconds. "Yes, I'm serious," she said. "Why? Are you really worried we might be thrown in jail and the bar closed?"

I don't think I admitted it to her that morning that her argument was stronger than mine, that she was right. The tenor of those times was not vindictive. People weren't suing each other all the time like they do now. Folks tried to be good neighbors and guys who had fought in Korea or gone through other hard times and ended up tending bar would hardly have been lying in wait to nail a couple of teenagers out for their first drink. In fact, they probably would have comped us kids a drink or two.

"Okay, I get it, I said. "I'll go with you but I think it's a bad idea and you've gotta promise me, Grace, that if the waiter gives us any shit about our ages or our licenses, we don't answer him and get into a big discussion, we just turn and walk out – briskly. Because between my dad and my school, I could get kicked out or suspended, okay? And I don't want that to happen – no way!"

"Good. So, when do you want to go?

"If we go now, it'll be lunch time when we get there."

We walked to my house to pick up my old four-door Plymouth and headed for town. "Let's go over what we have to memorize on our driver's licenses," I suggested. She agreed and read my false biographic information to me while I drove. A silence fell over us for a few minutes while she memorized her info and I thought of all the things that were at stake – my education, my whole life really. But there was no way out now.

Then, after a short pause to keep the mood from getting too serious I said, "You're going to do well in your criminal life. You'll probably become god mother of the O'Neil crime syndicate."

"Very funny," she said. "Okay, stick your new license in your wallet where your real license is so it'll look natural if you have to take it out for some reason," Grace instructed, "and put your real license in the glove compartment so you don't get them confused."

"Here, you do it. I'm driving." Grace busied herself with this chore. Finally, she took a deep breath and said, "Ready to go!" Excitement filled her voice.

"Easy there, girl," I said. "Where are we going?"

"No idea," she said. "I thought you had a bar in mind." After some discussion, we confessed that neither of us had been to a bar in town. We couldn't even come up with the name of a bar. So we cruised.

Soon enough I said, "Look! Just what we need." About one-half block ahead I spotted a yellow neon light tracing around and around the silhouette of a horse balanced on his hindquarters and kicking his forefeet high in the air.

"Yeah, let's give that one a try," Grace replied.

Finding parking in that part of town was no problem, but conjuring up a reason for being there, if our parents found out and asked, would be. I could feel my mood change from excited to anxious as we slid out of the car and locked the doors.

Side by side we began our walk to the Palomino Bar and Grille. "Are you sure you want to do this, G? It could run right off the tracks, you know."

"Yeah, it could, but that's what makes it a legitimate test. I understand your rock climber. He had to know that he'd be ready if faced with a life or death situation. Our test isn't nearly as severe as his, but it ain't a sure bet either. What about you?

"One hundred percent," I said, showing her a thumb's up but thinking 'Shit, I could have had a beer right there in Gracie's kitchen!'

Like the final scene in *High Noon*, the town, this part of it anyway, was deserted. It wasn't hot, but a bright sun hung overhead in a cloudless sky. I felt alone and on a fool's errand, but I had to go because I couldn't let the woman in my life see me walk away from trouble. As we approached the bar, we heard a new Elvis tune, *It's Now or Never*, wafting out an open window. I looked at Grace. "Good omen," she said. Agreed," I said, and pulled the door open for her.

Taking a step across the threshold of the Palomino and five or six more steps inside was transformative. The senses were overwhelmed by the smells of forty or so construction workers, stale beer, a never-before washed floor, and air so smoky I swear it was tactile. The patrons were all male. Most were wearing hard hats over their long hair, three-day growths of beard, heavy canvas pants, and metal-toed, thick-souled boots that wouldn't allow punctures by sharp objects. I was 5'5" about 130 pounds and probably looked like my mother had scrubbed my neck thoroughly before letting me out of the house.

The noise level prevented conversation, but I again put my face close to Gracie's and asked, "You okay?" Her eyes were the size of fried eggs and they were already watering profusely from the smoke. Her red and green plaid skirt and soft yellow Carroll Reed Shetland sweater made her look about 12 years old. The fact that she was squeezing my hand with all her might and had started to cough did nothing to enhance her image as a seasoned bar girl. But she was still spunky. In answer to my question she yelled to me, "Never better!"

We made our way to the bar, but the two bartenders were

very busy. After several minutes one spotted me waving at him. He had probably failed to see us because we were standing between two workers whose shoes must have weighed more than I did. The bartender, who had on a tight t-shirt, looked like a professional wrestler. He greeted me with a huge grin and said, "Merry Christmas. I'm Eric. Your first beer's on the house so what can I bring you?

"Well, thank you very much. Thanks. I'll have a Bud," I said,

"And your pretty little Sheila," he said, looking at Gracie, what'll you have, my dear?"

Grace was stunned and speechless. Since entering the Palomino, she had been mesmerized by the bar, its volume and its clients swirling in her head. She hadn't heard anything decipherable until the words "What'll you have" registered. Despite all the time and effort she had put into this illegal venture, she had not considered what she would order when that crucial moment arrived and since she had never ordered a drink, she had no experience to draw on. I gave her some time, too much perhaps, as it felt as if the three of us had been staring at each other for two hours when I finally said, "How about a beer, Grace?"

"No, no," she said, as she seemed to regain her consciousness. "Beer isn't festive enough. You go ahead and order, Honey," Grace said, tossing me the hot potato."

"I've ordered already, sweetie. How about champagne? We could have a nice toast with that." I was looking at her as I spoke, so I saw the answer to Eric's puzzler register on her face. In the blink of an eye her expression changed from consternation to relief.

Then her face brightened, she pointed a finger at the wrestler and said with authority, "Gimme a scotch and bourbon on the rocks, Eric."

ACKNOWLEDGEMENTS

To each of you I extend my thanks and gratitude for your contributions to this book and to me over the years.

John and Connie Adkins
Evan Daniels and Sue Freeman
Jeff Decker
Ed Dixon
Lew and Judy Eisenberg
John Fowler
Maria Lukowsky
Brent and Michelle Murphy
Snow Philip
David Smith
Sol Safran
Charles Tack
Ben and Julie Wickham
Bill and Mary Woolam

To Ben Kimball, the editor of all the stories in both my books, I owe a special thanks. Your edits and insights have been invaluable, Ben. Thanks.

And to my family, Ben, Byron, Karen, Patty, Rob, and Sharley, lots of love.

- Dad
Summer 2019

About the Author

R.K. Simpson lives in Alexandria, Virginia, with his wife Patty. He is a graduate of Dartmouth College and a veteran of the Marine Corps and the war in Vietnam. He served as a diplomat in several of our embassies in Europe and Africa for over twenty years. Upon retiring from the government, he worked as a pediatric nurse for fifteen years. He has three adult children.

The New Atlantian Library

NewAtlantianLibrary.com
or AbsolutelyAmazingEbooks.com
or AA-eBooks.com